We hope this book has been informative and helpful on your journey to understanding and celebrating older adults. Thank you for your interest and support!

AF498477

Title: The Golden Age of Meme Coins: Navigating the Pre-2017 Crypto Market
Subtitle: TrumpCoin, Pepecash, and other memetic currencies that paved the way for modern crypto

Series: The Rise of Meme Coins: Exploring the Pre-2017 Crypto Landscape
By Alexander C. Blair

Table of Contents

Introduction
Overview of cryptocurrencies

Cryptocurrencies have emerged as a revolutionary force within the financial landscape, introducing a decentralized and secure means of conducting transactions and storing value. In this chapter, we will provide an in-depth overview of cryptocurrencies, exploring their fundamental principles, underlying technologies, and the transformative impact they have had on various industries.

1. What are cryptocurrencies? Cryptocurrencies are digital or virtual currencies that employ cryptographic techniques to secure transactions and control the creation of new units. Unlike traditional fiat currencies, cryptocurrencies are not issued or regulated by any central authority, such as a government or financial institution. They rely on decentralized networks, typically based on blockchain technology, which enables transparency, immutability, and resistance to censorship.

2. The birth of Bitcoin Bitcoin, introduced in 2009 by the pseudonymous Satoshi Nakamoto, was the first decentralized cryptocurrency. It laid the foundation for the development of a new financial ecosystem, inspiring the creation of numerous other cryptocurrencies. Bitcoin's core principles, including peer-to-peer transactions, proof-of-work consensus mechanism, and limited supply, set the stage for the subsequent evolution of the crypto market.

3. Blockchain technology Blockchain, the underlying technology behind most cryptocurrencies, is a distributed ledger system that records transactions across multiple computers, or nodes. Each transaction is added to a "block" and linked to the previous blocks, forming an unalterable chain of information. Blockchain's immutability,

transparency, and decentralized nature provide the necessary trust and security for cryptocurrency transactions.

4. Different types of cryptocurrencies Cryptocurrencies can be categorized into several types, each serving unique purposes within the ecosystem. These include:

a. Currency coins: Bitcoin and other cryptocurrencies designed primarily as digital currencies for conducting transactions.

b. Platform coins: Cryptocurrencies that power decentralized platforms and enable the creation of decentralized applications (DApps).

c. Utility tokens: Tokens that grant access to specific services or products within a blockchain ecosystem.

d. Security tokens: Tokens that represent ownership in an underlying asset, such as real estate or company shares.

5. The rise of altcoins Following the success of Bitcoin, alternative cryptocurrencies, often referred to as "altcoins," began to emerge. These altcoins sought to address perceived limitations or introduce novel features that differentiated them from Bitcoin. Examples include Ethereum, Ripple, Litecoin, and many others. Altcoins played a pivotal role in expanding the functionality and diversity of the cryptocurrency market.

6. Cryptocurrency market dynamics The cryptocurrency market is characterized by its volatility, with prices fluctuating rapidly in response to various factors such as market demand, regulatory developments, technological advancements, and investor sentiment. Understanding the dynamics of the market, including factors that influence

price movements and market cycles, is crucial for navigating the cryptocurrency landscape.

7. Use cases and adoption Cryptocurrencies have found applications beyond mere financial transactions. They are being used for remittances, cross-border payments, decentralized finance (DeFi), non-fungible tokens (NFTs), and more. Governments, financial institutions, and tech companies are increasingly exploring the potential of blockchain technology and cryptocurrencies to streamline processes, enhance security, and foster innovation.

Conclusion In this chapter, we have provided a comprehensive overview of cryptocurrencies, exploring their origins, underlying technologies, and the diverse landscape they have created. Understanding the fundamental principles and dynamics of cryptocurrencies is essential for comprehending the unique context in which meme coins emerged before 2017. With this foundation in place, we can now delve into the captivating world of meme coins and their impact on the crypto market during what can be considered as the Golden Age of these distinctive digital assets.

Importance of understanding the history of cryptocurrencies

In order to grasp the full significance and impact of cryptocurrencies, it is crucial to delve into their rich history. By exploring the historical context, milestones, and key events, we can gain valuable insights into the evolution of cryptocurrencies and their current state. In this chapter, we will discuss the importance of understanding the history of cryptocurrencies and how it provides a foundation for comprehending their present and future implications.

1. Contextualizing the emergence of cryptocurrencies To truly understand cryptocurrencies, we must examine the factors that led to their creation. We will explore the shortcomings of traditional financial systems, such as centralized control, lack of transparency, and susceptibility to fraud. The rise of the internet and advancements in cryptography also played a vital role in laying the groundwork for the birth of cryptocurrencies.

2. Bitcoin: The genesis of a revolution The launch of Bitcoin in 2009 marked a groundbreaking moment in the history of cryptocurrencies. We will delve into the motivations behind Bitcoin's creation, including the desire for a decentralized currency and the need to address the flaws of traditional banking systems. Understanding Bitcoin's pioneering role and the principles it introduced is essential to grasp the broader cryptocurrency landscape.

3. Evolution of blockchain technology The development and refinement of blockchain technology have been instrumental in shaping the trajectory of cryptocurrencies. We will trace the evolution of blockchain from its humble beginnings as a supporting technology for Bitcoin to its application in various industries and sectors

beyond digital currencies. Exploring the technological advancements, challenges, and innovations within the blockchain space helps us appreciate the potential and limitations of cryptocurrencies.

4. Market cycles and lessons learned Cryptocurrencies have experienced significant market cycles characterized by both booms and busts. We will examine the notable market cycles, such as the 2013 Bitcoin rally and subsequent crash, as well as the meteoric rise and subsequent correction in 2017. Analyzing these cycles enables us to identify patterns, understand the dynamics of speculative bubbles, and gain insights into the factors that drive market sentiment.

5. Regulatory developments and industry challenges The history of cryptocurrencies is intertwined with regulatory developments and challenges. We will explore how governments and regulatory bodies have responded to the emergence of cryptocurrencies, from initial skepticism to subsequent efforts to establish regulatory frameworks. Understanding the regulatory landscape provides valuable context for assessing the risks and opportunities associated with cryptocurrencies.

6. Lessons from past failures and successes The history of cryptocurrencies is marked by notable successes and failures. We will examine the rise and fall of various cryptocurrencies, including those that were once highly valued but ultimately failed to maintain their prominence. Analyzing these case studies allows us to learn from past mistakes, identify key factors for success, and make informed decisions in the current crypto landscape.

7. Impact on the broader financial ecosystem Cryptocurrencies have not only disrupted traditional financial systems but have also catalyzed innovations in

areas such as decentralized finance (DeFi) and digital asset ownership. We will explore how cryptocurrencies have influenced the broader financial ecosystem, including the emergence of new financial instruments, the integration of blockchain in traditional industries, and the democratization of access to financial services.

Conclusion Understanding the history of cryptocurrencies is paramount to grasp the significance and potential of these digital assets. By examining the contextual factors, technological advancements, market cycles, regulatory landscape, and lessons learned, we gain a comprehensive understanding of the evolution of cryptocurrencies. This historical foundation will serve as a solid basis for exploring the unique phenomenon of meme coins that emerged before 2017, during what can be considered as the Golden Age of these distinct digital assets.

"The Golden Age of Meme Coins: Navigating the Pre-2017 Crypto Market" is a book that aims to shed light on the fascinating world of meme coins that emerged before 2017. In this chapter, we will explore the purpose and scope of the book, outlining the key objectives, target audience, and the unique value it offers to readers.

1. Objectives of the book The primary objective of this book is to provide a comprehensive exploration of the meme coins that gained popularity prior to 2017. By delving into the background, technical features, market performance, controversies, and unique aspects of each coin, we aim to offer readers a deep understanding of the significant meme coins that contributed to the early cryptocurrency landscape.

2. Target audience This book is intended for a wide range of individuals interested in cryptocurrencies, investing, and the cultural phenomenon surrounding meme coins. It caters to both newcomers seeking to learn about the historical context of cryptocurrencies and experienced cryptocurrency enthusiasts who wish to expand their knowledge and gain insights into the early meme coin market.

3. Unique value of the book "The Golden Age of Meme Coins" stands out from existing literature by focusing specifically on meme coins that emerged before 2017. While meme coins have gained significant attention in recent years, this book uncovers their early origins, offering readers a comprehensive understanding of their historical significance and the impact they had on the crypto market.

4. Historical context and analysis This book goes beyond the surface-level understanding of meme coins and provides readers with a deep dive into their historical

context. By analyzing the market dynamics, technological developments, regulatory landscape, and lessons learned from past successes and failures, readers will gain valuable insights that can inform their understanding of the current crypto landscape.

5. Exploration of unique features and controversies "The Golden Age of Meme Coins" aims to present a balanced examination of each meme coin's technical features, market performance, controversies, and criticisms. By exploring the controversies surrounding these coins, readers will gain a more nuanced understanding of the challenges faced by meme coins in their early stages and how they shaped the perception of this unique category within the broader cryptocurrency community.

6. Implications for the future of cryptocurrencies By studying the meme coins of the past, readers will be able to draw connections and implications for the present and future of cryptocurrencies. This book will explore the enduring influence of meme coins, their impact on cultural movements, and how the lessons learned from their history can inform the development and evolution of the crypto market going forward.

Conclusion The purpose of "The Golden Age of Meme Coins: Navigating the Pre-2017 Crypto Market" is to provide readers with a comprehensive understanding of the meme coins that emerged before 2017, their historical context, technical features, market performance, and controversies. By exploring these early meme coins, readers will gain valuable insights into the evolving cryptocurrency landscape and the cultural phenomena that have shaped it. Whether you are a newcomer or an experienced cryptocurrency enthusiast, this book aims to broaden your knowledge and equip you with the tools to navigate the ever-changing world of cryptocurrencies.

Chapter 1: TrumpCoin, SHA-256, launched in 2016, USD 4 million ATH in Feb 2017
Background and history of TrumpCoin

Introduction: In this chapter, we will delve into the background and history of TrumpCoin, one of the notable meme coins that emerged before 2017. TrumpCoin, named after the 45th President of the United States, Donald J. Trump, gained attention for its unique branding and aspirations. We will explore the motivations behind its creation, the community that supported it, and the impact it had on the crypto market.

1. The inspiration behind TrumpCoin: TrumpCoin was launched during the 2016 U.S. presidential election, a time of intense political polarization and fervent support for Donald Trump. We will discuss the factors that motivated the creation of TrumpCoin, including the desire to show support for Trump's policies and to capitalize on his popularity among certain segments of the population.

2. The TrumpCoin community: TrumpCoin attracted a passionate community of supporters who believed in its mission and vision. We will explore the dynamics of this community, their motivations for getting involved, and the role they played in promoting and advocating for TrumpCoin.

3. Key features and branding: TrumpCoin distinguished itself through its unique branding and marketing. We will examine the key features of TrumpCoin, including its underlying technology, SHA-256, and the specific attributes that differentiated it from other cryptocurrencies.

4. Initial coin offering (ICO): The launch of TrumpCoin was accompanied by an initial coin offering

(ICO), a crowdfunding method used by many cryptocurrency projects. We will discuss the details of TrumpCoin's ICO, including the fundraising goals, distribution of tokens, and the response from the crypto community.

5. Market performance and controversies: TrumpCoin experienced significant volatility in terms of its market performance. We will analyze the price fluctuations, trading volumes, and the factors that influenced its valuation. Additionally, we will explore any controversies or criticisms surrounding TrumpCoin, such as allegations of pump-and-dump schemes or the politicization of a cryptocurrency project.

6. Community initiatives and impact: Beyond its price and market dynamics, TrumpCoin aimed to support charitable initiatives aligned with the values of the Trump administration. We will highlight the community-driven projects and philanthropic efforts associated with TrumpCoin and discuss their impact on the crypto community and society at large.

7. Legacy and lessons learned: As with any cryptocurrency project, TrumpCoin's story offers valuable insights and lessons. We will reflect on the legacy of TrumpCoin, its impact on the broader crypto market, and the lessons that can be drawn from its history, including the intersection of politics and cryptocurrencies.

Conclusion: The background and history of TrumpCoin provide a fascinating case study within the realm of meme coins that emerged before 2017. By understanding its origins, community dynamics, market performance, and controversies, we gain a deeper understanding of the complexities and nuances of the meme coin phenomenon. As we move forward, the story of TrumpCoin serves as a reminder of the intersection between cryptocurrency and politics and the unique narratives that can shape the crypto landscape.

Technical features of SHA-256

Introduction: In this section, we will explore the technical features of SHA-256, the underlying cryptographic algorithm used by TrumpCoin and many other cryptocurrencies. Understanding the technical aspects of SHA-256 is crucial for comprehending the security, efficiency, and functionality of TrumpCoin. We will delve into the workings of SHA-256, its cryptographic properties, and its relevance to the broader cryptocurrency ecosystem.

1. Cryptographic hash functions: To understand SHA-256, we must first grasp the concept of cryptographic hash functions. We will explain the purpose and characteristics of cryptographic hash functions, which are essential components of many cryptographic systems. Their properties include collision resistance, pre-image resistance, and computational efficiency.

2. SHA-256 overview: SHA-256 (Secure Hash Algorithm 256-bit) is a member of the SHA-2 (Secure Hash Algorithm 2) family of cryptographic hash functions. We will provide an overview of SHA-256, discussing its design principles, key properties, and intended applications. SHA-256 is widely used in various cryptographic applications, including digital signatures, password hashing, and blockchain technology.

3. Data processing in SHA-256: We will explore the step-by-step process of data processing in SHA-256. This includes message padding, message block division, and the main stages of the SHA-256 algorithm: message schedule, compression function, and hash value computation. Understanding these stages helps to comprehend how data is transformed and secured within the SHA-256 algorithm.

4. Collision resistance: One of the fundamental properties of cryptographic hash functions is collision resistance, which ensures that it is computationally infeasible to find two different inputs that produce the same hash output. We will discuss the collision resistance of SHA-256, its implications for the security of TrumpCoin, and the significance of this property in the broader cryptographic context.

5. Security considerations: We will delve into the security aspects of SHA-256 and its relevance to TrumpCoin. This includes discussions on the resistance against cryptographic attacks, such as pre-image attacks, birthday attacks, and length extension attacks. By understanding the security features and limitations of SHA-256, readers can evaluate the robustness of TrumpCoin's underlying cryptographic foundation.

6. Performance and efficiency: SHA-256 is designed to provide a balance between security and efficiency. We will discuss the performance characteristics of SHA-256, including its computational complexity, memory requirements, and throughput. Understanding the efficiency of SHA-256 helps to assess the practicality of using this cryptographic algorithm in real-world applications such as TrumpCoin.

7. SHA-256 in the broader cryptocurrency ecosystem: SHA-256 has had a significant impact on the cryptocurrency landscape beyond its use in TrumpCoin. We will explore the broader adoption of SHA-256 in notable cryptocurrencies like Bitcoin and discuss the implications for interoperability, security, and mining. This discussion will provide a context for understanding the role of SHA-256 in the evolution of cryptocurrencies.

Conclusion: The technical features of SHA-256 play a crucial role in the functionality and security of TrumpCoin and many other cryptocurrencies. By understanding the workings of SHA-256, its cryptographic properties, and its relevance to the broader cryptocurrency ecosystem, readers gain insights into the underlying technology that powers meme coins and the broader crypto market. As we move forward, the technical foundation provided by SHA-256 continues to shape the development and innovation within the cryptocurrency space.

Launch of TrumpCoin in 2016

Introduction: In this section, we will explore the launch of TrumpCoin, a meme coin named after the 45th President of the United States, Donald J. Trump. The launch of TrumpCoin in 2016 was a significant milestone in the early meme coin landscape, attracting attention and enthusiasm from both cryptocurrency enthusiasts and Trump supporters. We will delve into the details of the launch, including the motivation behind its creation, the development process, and the community's response.

1. Motivation for creating TrumpCoin: The creation of TrumpCoin was driven by several motivations. We will discuss the factors that led to the inception of TrumpCoin, including the desire to show support for Donald Trump's political agenda, capitalize on his popularity, and create a unique cryptocurrency project that aligned with the ethos of the Trump movement.

2. Development and planning: The launch of TrumpCoin required careful planning and development. We will explore the process of creating TrumpCoin, including the selection of the SHA-256 cryptographic algorithm, the design of the blockchain infrastructure, and the considerations involved in ensuring the security and functionality of the coin. Additionally, we will discuss the role of the development team and their contributions to the project.

3. Initial Coin Offering (ICO): To fund the development and promotion of TrumpCoin, an initial coin offering (ICO) was conducted. We will delve into the details of the TrumpCoin ICO, including the fundraising goals, the distribution of tokens, and the mechanisms used to attract investors. The ICO served as a crucial phase in generating initial interest and financial support for the project.

4. Community engagement and marketing: The success of TrumpCoin relied heavily on community engagement and marketing efforts. We will explore the strategies employed to promote and create awareness about TrumpCoin, such as social media campaigns, online forums, and partnerships. The active involvement of the community played a pivotal role in spreading the word about TrumpCoin and attracting new participants.

5. Listing on cryptocurrency exchanges: To ensure liquidity and accessibility, TrumpCoin needed to be listed on cryptocurrency exchanges. We will discuss the process of getting TrumpCoin listed on exchanges, including the challenges faced, the negotiation process, and the impact of exchange listings on the coin's market performance. The availability of TrumpCoin on exchanges was crucial for investors and traders interested in acquiring or trading the coin.

6. Reception and early market performance: Upon its launch, TrumpCoin received varying degrees of reception from the cryptocurrency community. We will examine the initial market performance of TrumpCoin, including factors that influenced its price, trading volumes, and market capitalization. This analysis will provide insights into the early dynamics and investor sentiment surrounding TrumpCoin.

7. Evolution and updates: After the initial launch, TrumpCoin underwent evolution and updates to enhance its functionality and address any technical or community-related issues. We will discuss the major updates or milestones in the development of TrumpCoin, highlighting how the project evolved over time and adapted to the changing cryptocurrency landscape.

Conclusion: The launch of TrumpCoin in 2016 marked a significant moment in the early meme coin era. By exploring the motivations behind its creation, the development and planning process, the ICO, community engagement, exchange listings, and early market performance, readers gain a comprehensive understanding of the launch phase of TrumpCoin. The launch set the stage for TrumpCoin's journey and laid the foundation for its subsequent impact on the cryptocurrency market.

Market performance of TrumpCoin

Introduction: In this section, we will explore the market performance of TrumpCoin, examining its price dynamics, trading volumes, market capitalization, and the factors that influenced its value. Understanding the market performance of TrumpCoin provides insights into the reception of the coin by investors and the broader cryptocurrency community. We will analyze key milestones, notable price movements, and the impact of external factors on TrumpCoin's market performance.

1. Initial price discovery: After its launch, TrumpCoin entered a phase of price discovery, during which the market determined its initial value. We will discuss the factors that influenced the early price of TrumpCoin, including investor sentiment, trading activity, and the supply and demand dynamics within the market. Additionally, we will analyze the role of exchanges and their impact on the price discovery process.

2. Volatility and price fluctuations: Like many cryptocurrencies, TrumpCoin experienced significant volatility in its early stages. We will examine the price fluctuations and the factors that contributed to the volatility of TrumpCoin, such as market speculation, news events, and overall market sentiment. This analysis will provide insights into the risk and potential reward associated with investing in TrumpCoin during its early phases.

3. All-time high (ATH) and ATH analysis: TrumpCoin reached a notable all-time high (ATH) in February 2017, achieving a market capitalization of USD 4 million. We will analyze the factors that led to this peak, including any significant events, community-driven initiatives, or external factors that contributed to the surge in TrumpCoin's value.

Furthermore, we will explore the impact of the ATH on the perception of TrumpCoin within the cryptocurrency community.

4. Corrections and price retracements: Following the ATH, TrumpCoin experienced price corrections and retracements. We will examine the retracement patterns, the extent of the price corrections, and the factors that triggered these market adjustments. Understanding these corrections provides insights into the market dynamics and the overall sentiment surrounding TrumpCoin.

5. Trading volumes and liquidity: The trading volumes and liquidity of TrumpCoin played a crucial role in its market performance. We will analyze the trading volumes of TrumpCoin, discussing the liquidity challenges faced by the coin and the impact on its price stability. Additionally, we will explore the factors that influenced trading volumes, such as community engagement, exchange listings, and market speculation.

6. Community sentiment and impact on the market: The sentiment and engagement of the TrumpCoin community had a significant influence on its market performance. We will discuss the role of community-driven initiatives, social media activity, and community sentiment in shaping the perception of TrumpCoin within the broader cryptocurrency market. Additionally, we will explore any notable community-led projects or initiatives that impacted the market performance of TrumpCoin.

7. External factors and market correlation: The market performance of TrumpCoin was also influenced by external factors that affected the broader cryptocurrency market. We will analyze the correlation between TrumpCoin's price movements and market trends, including

the impact of regulatory developments, geopolitical events, and the performance of major cryptocurrencies. Understanding these external factors provides a broader context for interpreting TrumpCoin's market performance.

Conclusion: The market performance of TrumpCoin reflected the reception and sentiment of investors and the cryptocurrency community. By analyzing the initial price discovery, volatility, ATH, price corrections, trading volumes, community sentiment, and the impact of external factors, readers gain insights into the dynamics and factors that shaped TrumpCoin's market journey. The market performance of TrumpCoin provides valuable lessons and insights for investors and enthusiasts in understanding the complexities of the cryptocurrency market.

Controversies and criticisms surrounding TrumpCoin

Introduction: In this section, we will explore the controversies and criticisms surrounding TrumpCoin, a meme coin inspired by the 45th President of the United States, Donald J. Trump. While TrumpCoin gained popularity and attracted a dedicated community, it also faced various controversies and criticisms from both within and outside the cryptocurrency community. We will delve into the key controversies, criticisms, and debates that emerged during TrumpCoin's existence, providing a comprehensive analysis of the challenges and concerns associated with the coin.

1. Political implications and ideological divisions: Given its association with Donald Trump, TrumpCoin naturally carried political implications. We will examine the ideological divisions that emerged within the cryptocurrency community regarding TrumpCoin's political affiliation and the extent to which these divisions affected the perception and adoption of the coin. The political nature of TrumpCoin made it a subject of heated debates and discussions, often leading to controversies.

2. Accuracy of claims and use of Trump's image: One of the controversies surrounding TrumpCoin revolved around the accuracy of claims made by its proponents. We will discuss the accuracy of statements and promises made about the coin's purpose, functionality, and contributions to Trump's political agenda. Additionally, we will explore the use of Trump's image and the legal and ethical implications associated with leveraging a public figure's likeness for a cryptocurrency project.

3. Scams and fraudulent activities: Like many cryptocurrencies, TrumpCoin became a target for scammers and fraudulent activities. We will examine the instances of scams, phishing attempts, and fraudulent schemes associated with TrumpCoin, including fake giveaways, pump-and-dump schemes, and unauthorized fundraising campaigns. Analyzing these incidents sheds light on the challenges and risks faced by investors and the broader cryptocurrency community.

4. Lack of transparency and governance: Critics of TrumpCoin raised concerns about the lack of transparency and governance within the project. We will explore the criticisms related to the transparency of the development team, decision-making processes, and the allocation of funds raised during the initial coin offering (ICO). This discussion will address the importance of transparency and accountability in cryptocurrency projects.

5. Regulatory scrutiny and compliance: TrumpCoin, like many cryptocurrencies, operated in a regulatory gray area. We will examine the regulatory scrutiny faced by TrumpCoin and the compliance challenges associated with its operation. This includes discussions on potential legal implications, compliance with financial regulations, and the efforts made by the TrumpCoin team to navigate the evolving regulatory landscape.

6. Market manipulation and price volatility: Another criticism surrounding TrumpCoin relates to market manipulation and price volatility. We will explore allegations of market manipulation, including pump-and-dump schemes, coordinated trading activities, and artificial inflation of trading volumes. Understanding the impact of market manipulation on TrumpCoin's price dynamics

provides insights into the challenges faced by meme coins in maintaining a stable and reliable market.

7. Community disputes and fragmentation: The TrumpCoin community experienced internal disputes and fragmentation, leading to divisions and conflicts among its members. We will discuss the factors that contributed to community disputes, including disagreements over project direction, governance issues, and ideological differences. Analyzing these community challenges highlights the importance of fostering a cohesive and inclusive community for the success and sustainability of a cryptocurrency project.

Conclusion: TrumpCoin faced its fair share of controversies and criticisms throughout its existence. By examining the political implications, accuracy of claims, scams and fraudulent activities, transparency and governance issues, regulatory scrutiny, market manipulation, and community disputes, readers gain a comprehensive understanding of the challenges and criticisms faced by TrumpCoin. This analysis serves as a reminder of the complexities and risks associated with meme coins and highlights the importance of due diligence and critical evaluation when engaging with such projects.

Introduction: In this section, we will explore the background and history of Pepecash, a meme coin built on the Counterparty platform. Pepecash gained significant attention and popularity within the cryptocurrency community, primarily due to its association with Pepe the Frog, an internet meme. We will delve into the origins of Pepecash, its development, and the factors that contributed to its rise as a prominent meme coin.

1. The rise of internet memes: To understand the context of Pepecash, it is essential to explore the rise of internet memes and their influence on popular culture. We will discuss the emergence of Pepe the Frog as an iconic internet meme, its evolution, and the significance of memes in shaping online communities. This discussion provides a foundation for understanding the cultural impact and relevance of Pepecash.

2. Origins of Pepecash: We will delve into the origins of Pepecash, examining the individuals or community behind its creation and the motivations that led to its inception. Understanding the background of Pepecash sheds light on the intentions and vision behind the coin and provides insights into the unique aspects that set it apart from other cryptocurrencies.

3. Introduction of Counterparty: Counterparty, the platform on which Pepecash was built, played a crucial role in its development and functionality. We will provide an overview of Counterparty, discussing its features, capabilities, and its positioning within the broader cryptocurrency ecosystem. This discussion will highlight the

technical foundation on which Pepecash was built and its implications for the coin's functionality.

4. Pepecash's role in the meme economy: Pepecash found its place within the meme economy, a concept that emerged as internet memes gained cultural and financial significance. We will explore the dynamics of the meme economy, the role of cryptocurrencies within this ecosystem, and the unique contribution of Pepecash to this growing phenomenon. This analysis will shed light on the broader implications of meme coins in the context of internet culture and digital assets.

5. Community and adoption: Pepecash developed a dedicated community that actively participated in its growth and adoption. We will examine the community dynamics surrounding Pepecash, including the efforts made by the community to promote and support the coin. This discussion will explore community-driven initiatives, social media engagement, and the role of influencers in spreading awareness and driving adoption of Pepecash.

6. Use cases and applications: Beyond its status as a meme coin, Pepecash demonstrated various use cases and applications within the cryptocurrency ecosystem. We will discuss the practical applications of Pepecash, including its use in digital art, collectibles, decentralized exchanges, and other innovative projects. Exploring the use cases of Pepecash highlights its versatility and potential as a digital asset beyond its meme origins.

7. Evolution and future developments: Pepecash experienced evolution and ongoing developments over time. We will discuss the key milestones and updates in the development of Pepecash, including technological advancements, governance improvements, and the

introduction of new features. Additionally, we will explore the future prospects and potential challenges for Pepecash, considering the evolving landscape of meme coins and the cryptocurrency industry.

Conclusion: The background and history of Pepecash provide valuable insights into the emergence and growth of a meme coin within the cryptocurrency ecosystem. By examining the rise of internet memes, the origins of Pepecash, the role of Counterparty, the coin's involvement in the meme economy, community dynamics, use cases, and future developments, readers gain a comprehensive understanding of Pepecash's journey. This analysis contributes to the broader knowledge of meme coins and their significance in the evolving landscape of cryptocurrencies.

Technical features of Counterparty

Introduction: In this section, we will explore the technical features of Counterparty, the platform on which Pepecash was built. Counterparty is a decentralized protocol that enables the creation and execution of smart contracts on the Bitcoin blockchain. Understanding the technical aspects of Counterparty is crucial for comprehending the functionality and capabilities of Pepecash as a meme coin. We will delve into the key technical features and innovations of Counterparty, shedding light on its role in the development and success of Pepecash.

1. Integration with the Bitcoin blockchain: Counterparty is built on top of the Bitcoin blockchain, leveraging its security and infrastructure. We will discuss the integration of Counterparty with Bitcoin, exploring the benefits and implications of utilizing the Bitcoin blockchain for smart contract functionality. This integration enables Pepecash and other tokens on Counterparty to inherit the security and immutability of the Bitcoin network.

2. Token creation and issuance: Counterparty allows users to create and issue tokens, including Pepecash, on the Bitcoin blockchain. We will explore the process of token creation and issuance on Counterparty, including the technical steps involved, such as creating a token name, determining the token supply, and defining additional properties and functionalities. This discussion will provide insights into the flexibility and customization options available for token creators.

3. Smart contracts and decentralized applications: Counterparty introduces smart contract functionality to the Bitcoin ecosystem, enabling the creation and execution of programmable agreements. We will delve into the technical

aspects of smart contracts on Counterparty, discussing the scripting language used, the execution model, and the capabilities for creating decentralized applications (DApps). This exploration will showcase the potential applications and innovations made possible by Counterparty's smart contract capabilities.

4. Decentralized exchange functionality: Counterparty features a built-in decentralized exchange (DEX) that allows users to trade tokens directly on the Counterparty platform. We will examine the technical aspects of the decentralized exchange, including the order matching process, the role of atomic swaps, and the integration with the underlying Bitcoin blockchain. This discussion will provide a deeper understanding of the trading mechanisms and liquidity options available to Pepecash holders.

5. Security and consensus mechanisms: Counterparty utilizes the Bitcoin blockchain's security infrastructure, including its proof-of-work consensus mechanism. We will explore the security measures implemented by Counterparty to ensure the integrity of transactions and the protection of user assets. This includes discussions on transaction confirmations, block validation, and potential vulnerabilities or attack vectors specific to the Counterparty protocol.

6. Integration with existing Bitcoin wallets: Counterparty allows users to interact with the protocol using existing Bitcoin wallets, simplifying the user experience and enhancing accessibility. We will discuss the technical aspects of integrating Counterparty with Bitcoin wallets, including the use of multi-signature addresses, wallet compatibility, and the benefits of leveraging existing wallet infrastructure for Pepecash transactions.

7. Scalability and future developments: Counterparty, like many blockchain platforms, faces challenges related to scalability and throughput. We will explore the current scalability limitations of Counterparty and discuss ongoing research and development efforts to address these challenges. Additionally, we will highlight potential future developments and upgrades that may enhance the technical capabilities of Counterparty and subsequently benefit Pepecash and other tokens built on the platform.

Conclusion: Understanding the technical features of Counterparty is essential for comprehending the underlying infrastructure and functionality of Pepecash as a meme coin. By examining Counterparty's integration with the Bitcoin blockchain, token creation and issuance, smart contract functionality, decentralized exchange capabilities, security measures, wallet integration, scalability challenges, and future developments, readers gain a comprehensive understanding of the technical foundations that enable the existence and operation of Pepecash and other tokens on the Counterparty platform. It provides insights into the decentralized nature of Pepecash, the programmability of smart contracts, and the opportunities for token creation and trading within the Counterparty ecosystem.

Moreover, understanding the technical features of Counterparty allows readers to appreciate the security measures in place, ensuring the integrity of transactions and protecting user assets. The integration with the Bitcoin blockchain enhances the robustness and immutability of Pepecash, leveraging the proven infrastructure and consensus mechanisms of Bitcoin.

Additionally, exploring the scalability challenges and future developments of Counterparty sheds light on the potential improvements and innovations that may further enhance Pepecash's technical capabilities. As the blockchain industry evolves, Counterparty's ongoing research and development efforts aim to address scalability concerns and introduce optimizations to enable a more efficient and scalable platform.

In conclusion, a thorough understanding of the technical features of Counterparty is crucial for comprehending the inner workings and possibilities of Pepecash as a meme coin. By examining its integration with the Bitcoin blockchain, smart contract functionality, decentralized exchange capabilities, security measures, wallet integration, scalability challenges, and future developments, readers gain a holistic understanding of the technical foundations that empower Pepecash and contribute to its position within the cryptocurrency ecosystem.

Launch of Pepecash in 2016

Introduction: In this section, we will explore the launch of Pepecash, a meme coin built on the Counterparty platform, in 2016. The launch of Pepecash marked the beginning of its journey within the cryptocurrency ecosystem and its subsequent rise to prominence. We will delve into the events leading up to the launch, the process of introducing Pepecash to the market, and the initial response from the crypto community. Understanding the launch of Pepecash provides valuable insights into the early stages of its development and sets the stage for its subsequent success.

1. Origins and motivations: To understand the launch of Pepecash, it is important to explore the origins and motivations behind its creation. We will discuss the individuals or community responsible for the development of Pepecash and their vision for the coin. This discussion will shed light on the initial intentions and goals set forth by the creators and their aspirations for Pepecash as a meme coin.

2. Pre-launch preparations: Before the official launch of Pepecash, various preparations were made to ensure a successful introduction to the market. We will examine the steps taken by the development team, such as code development, testing, and community building. Additionally, we will explore the marketing and promotional strategies employed to generate interest and awareness among potential users and investors.

3. Token distribution and initial coin offering (ICO): The distribution of Pepecash tokens played a crucial role in its launch. We will discuss the token distribution model implemented by the Pepecash team, including any pre-mining or allocation mechanisms. Furthermore, we will explore the process of the initial coin offering (ICO) for

Pepecash, analyzing the fundraising goals, the token sale structure, and the participation of early investors. This discussion will provide insights into the distribution dynamics and the initial market supply of Pepecash.

4. Early adoption and community response: The success of any cryptocurrency relies heavily on its adoption within the community. We will explore the early adoption of Pepecash, examining the response from the crypto community, including users, investors, and enthusiasts. This discussion will encompass the initial trading volume, market sentiment, and any notable endorsements or partnerships that contributed to the early success and visibility of Pepecash.

5. Market performance and price discovery: Following its launch, Pepecash entered the market, and its price began to fluctuate based on supply and demand dynamics. We will analyze the market performance of Pepecash, exploring its price discovery process, trading volume, and any significant price movements or milestones achieved during the initial stages. This analysis will provide insights into the early valuation and market perception of Pepecash as a meme coin.

6. Community engagement and development updates: Pepecash's launch was not only about introducing the coin to the market but also about fostering an active and engaged community. We will discuss the community engagement efforts undertaken by the Pepecash team, such as community forums, social media presence, and regular development updates. Additionally, we will examine how the community's feedback and involvement influenced the future development and direction of Pepecash.

7. Lessons learned and future directions: Reflecting on the launch of Pepecash, we will explore the lessons learned by the development team and the broader crypto community. We will analyze the successes, challenges, and notable experiences from Pepecash's launch, drawing insights that can be applied to future cryptocurrency launches. Furthermore, we will discuss the future directions envisioned for Pepecash, including planned updates, partnerships, and community-driven initiatives.

Conclusion: The launch of Pepecash in 2016 marked the beginning of its journey as an influential meme coin within the cryptocurrency ecosystem. By exploring the origins and motivations behind Pepecash, the pre-launch preparations, token distribution, early adoption, market performance, community engagement, and future directions, we gain a comprehensive understanding of the factors that contributed to its initial success.

The launch of Pepecash demonstrated the potential for meme coins to capture the imagination of the crypto community and attract widespread attention. It tapped into the growing interest in digital assets with a unique twist, leveraging the power of memes and internet culture. The success of Pepecash's launch served as a catalyst for the broader adoption of meme coins, paving the way for subsequent projects to explore the creative and expressive possibilities of the blockchain.

Throughout its launch, Pepecash also highlighted the importance of community engagement and active participation. The enthusiasm and support of the early adopters played a crucial role in establishing a vibrant and dedicated community around Pepecash. The development team's commitment to regular updates and open communication fostered trust and transparency, further solidifying the coin's position within the crypto landscape.

The launch of Pepecash also revealed valuable lessons for future meme coin projects and cryptocurrency launches in general. It emphasized the significance of thorough pre-launch preparations, including robust code development, rigorous testing, and effective marketing strategies. Furthermore, the experience of Pepecash shed light on the importance of striking a balance between community-driven initiatives and the need for a clear development roadmap to ensure long-term sustainability and growth.

Looking ahead, the launch of Pepecash set the stage for its continued evolution and exploration of new possibilities. The initial success and market response served as validation for its unique approach, attracting attention from both crypto enthusiasts and mainstream media. The lessons learned from Pepecash's launch continue to influence the development and launch strategies of subsequent meme coins, fueling innovation and creativity within the cryptocurrency space.

In conclusion, the launch of Pepecash in 2016 marked the beginning of its journey as an influential meme coin. By examining its origins, pre-launch preparations, token distribution, early adoption, market performance, community engagement, and future directions, we gain a comprehensive understanding of the factors that contributed to its initial success and the broader impact it had on the meme coin phenomenon within the cryptocurrency ecosystem.

Market performance of Pepecash

Introduction: The market performance of Pepecash played a crucial role in establishing its position within the cryptocurrency ecosystem. In this section, we will delve into the various aspects of Pepecash's market performance, including price movements, trading volume, market capitalization, and overall market sentiment. Understanding the market dynamics and factors that influenced the performance of Pepecash provides valuable insights into its journey as a meme coin and its reception within the crypto community.

1. Early price movements and volatility: Following its launch, Pepecash experienced initial price movements and volatility. We will analyze the early price chart of Pepecash, examining its fluctuations, price discovery process, and any notable price milestones achieved during the early stages. This analysis will shed light on the market sentiment and initial trading activity surrounding Pepecash, providing a foundation for understanding its subsequent performance.

2. Factors influencing market sentiment: Numerous factors can influence the market sentiment of a cryptocurrency, and Pepecash is no exception. We will explore the factors that played a significant role in shaping the market sentiment around Pepecash. This includes media coverage, community engagement, partnerships, regulatory developments, and broader market trends. Understanding these factors will help contextualize Pepecash's market performance and its positioning within the cryptocurrency landscape.

3. Trading volume and liquidity: The trading volume and liquidity of Pepecash are essential indicators of market activity and investor interest. We will analyze the trading

volume trends of Pepecash, examining its daily, weekly, and monthly trading activity. Additionally, we will explore the liquidity of Pepecash across different cryptocurrency exchanges, evaluating the availability of trading pairs and the ease of buying and selling Pepecash. This analysis will provide insights into the liquidity profile and market depth of Pepecash.

4. Market capitalization and ranking: Market capitalization is a widely used metric to assess the relative value and popularity of cryptocurrencies. We will explore the market capitalization of Pepecash, analyzing its growth and ranking among other cryptocurrencies. This discussion will encompass Pepecash's journey in terms of market capitalization, its position in the market cap rankings, and any notable fluctuations or milestones achieved during its peak performance.

5. Investor sentiment and community engagement: The sentiment of investors and the level of community engagement can greatly impact the market performance of a cryptocurrency. We will examine the sentiment surrounding Pepecash, analyzing social media discussions, community forums, and other platforms where Pepecash holders and enthusiasts gather. Additionally, we will explore the role of community engagement initiatives, such as meetups, conferences, and online events, in driving Pepecash's market performance.

6. Influences from the broader crypto market: The performance of Pepecash cannot be analyzed in isolation from the broader cryptocurrency market. We will explore the influences and correlations between Pepecash's market performance and the overall trends and developments in the crypto market. This includes analyzing the impact of major

market events, regulatory decisions, and technological advancements on the performance of Pepecash.

7. Impact of partnerships and collaborations: Partnerships and collaborations can significantly impact the market performance of a cryptocurrency. We will examine any notable partnerships or collaborations involving Pepecash, analyzing their influence on its market sentiment and trading activity. This discussion will shed light on the strategic alliances formed by Pepecash and how they contributed to its market performance.

Conclusion: The market performance of Pepecash played a pivotal role in establishing its position within the cryptocurrency ecosystem. By analyzing the early price movements and volatility, understanding the factors influencing market sentiment, evaluating trading volume and liquidity, examining market capitalization and ranking, assessing investor sentiment and community engagement, and considering influences from the broader crypto market and partnerships, we gain a comprehensive understanding of Pepecash's market performance.

The early price movements and volatility of Pepecash reflected the initial excitement and speculation surrounding the meme coin. As with many cryptocurrencies, Pepecash experienced periods of rapid price appreciation and significant price corrections. Analyzing these price movements provides insights into the market sentiment and the dynamics of supply and demand within the Pepecash ecosystem.

Various factors influenced the market sentiment surrounding Pepecash. Media coverage, both positive and negative, had a significant impact on how Pepecash was perceived by the wider crypto community. Positive media attention highlighted the innovative nature of Pepecash as a meme coin and its potential for disruption, while negative coverage raised concerns about the speculative nature of the project.

Trading volume and liquidity are crucial indicators of market activity and investor interest. Pepecash's trading volume reflected the level of engagement and participation from traders and investors. Higher trading volumes indicated increased market activity and liquidity, providing opportunities for traders to buy and sell Pepecash with ease.

Market capitalization and ranking provided a measure of Pepecash's value and its standing relative to other cryptocurrencies. Pepecash's market capitalization fluctuated over time, influenced by factors such as investor sentiment, market trends, and developments within the meme coin sector. A higher market capitalization indicated a larger market value and greater investor confidence in the project.

Investor sentiment and community engagement played a crucial role in shaping Pepecash's market performance. Positive sentiment and active community involvement contributed to increased demand and adoption of Pepecash. Community-driven initiatives, such as the creation of Pepe-themed digital collectibles and artwork, further enhanced the visibility and appeal of Pepecash within the crypto art community.

Pepecash's market performance was also influenced by broader market trends and developments in the crypto industry. Major market events, regulatory decisions, and technological advancements had an impact on investor sentiment and the overall performance of Pepecash. Additionally, partnerships and collaborations with other projects and platforms played a role in expanding Pepecash's reach and attracting new users and investors.

In conclusion, the market performance of Pepecash was shaped by various factors, including price movements, trading volume, market capitalization, investor sentiment, and community engagement. By analyzing these aspects, we gain insights into Pepecash's reception within the crypto community, its positioning within the broader market, and the factors that contributed to its success as a meme coin. Understanding the market performance of Pepecash provides valuable lessons for future meme coin projects and offers a glimpse into the evolving landscape of cryptocurrencies and digital assets.

Role of Pepecash in the crypto art community

Introduction: Pepecash, with its unique origins as a meme coin, has carved out a distinctive niche within the crypto art community. In this section, we will explore the role of Pepecash in the world of crypto art, examining how it has empowered artists, facilitated the creation and trading of digital collectibles, and fostered a vibrant ecosystem of creativity and collaboration. Understanding the significance of Pepecash in the crypto art community provides insights into the intersection of digital art, blockchain technology, and decentralized finance.

1. Empowering artists: Pepecash has played a significant role in empowering artists to monetize their digital creations and gain recognition within the crypto art space. We will delve into the ways in which Pepecash has provided opportunities for artists to tokenize their artwork, create limited edition digital collectibles, and establish a direct relationship with their audience. This empowerment has challenged traditional art market dynamics and opened up new avenues for artists to showcase and sell their work.

2. Tokenization of digital art: Pepecash's integration with the Counterparty platform has enabled the tokenization of digital art, allowing artists to transform their creations into unique digital assets. We will explore how Pepecash has facilitated the tokenization process, including the creation, issuance, and distribution of digital art tokens. This discussion will cover the technical aspects of tokenization, such as the use of non-fungible tokens (NFTs) and smart contracts, as well as the benefits and challenges associated with the tokenization of art.

3. Creation and trading of digital collectibles: Pepecash has become synonymous with the creation and

trading of digital collectibles, also known as "Pepe-themed" assets. We will examine the phenomenon of Pepe-themed digital collectibles, exploring their popularity, rarity, and cultural significance within the crypto art community. Additionally, we will delve into the platforms and marketplaces where these digital collectibles are traded, highlighting the role of Pepecash as the medium of exchange for these unique assets.

4. Collaborative projects and communities: Pepecash has fostered a vibrant ecosystem of collaboration and community engagement within the crypto art space. We will explore the various collaborative projects that have emerged around Pepecash, such as art contests, auctions, and community-driven initiatives. These collaborative efforts have not only enriched the Pepecash ecosystem but have also created opportunities for artists and collectors to connect, collaborate, and showcase their work to a broader audience.

5. Fusion of art and technology: Pepecash's presence in the crypto art community represents the fusion of art and technology. We will examine how the decentralized and transparent nature of blockchain technology has transformed the way art is created, displayed, and valued. This discussion will encompass topics such as provenance, ownership verification, and the potential for new business models enabled by blockchain technology. Pepecash's role in this fusion serves as a testament to the transformative power of crypto art.

6. Challenges and future prospects: While Pepecash has made significant strides in the crypto art community, it also faces challenges and uncertainties. We will discuss the challenges related to copyright infringement, the sustainability of the market for Pepe-themed digital

collectibles, and the need for continued innovation and development within the Pepecash ecosystem. Furthermore, we will explore the future prospects for Pepecash and its potential to continue shaping the crypto art landscape.

Conclusion: Pepecash has emerged as a significant player within the crypto art community, empowering artists, driving the tokenization of digital art, facilitating the creation and trading of digital collectibles, and fostering collaborative projects and communities. By understanding the role of Pepecash in the crypto art community, we gain insights into the evolving landscape of digital art and its intersection with blockchain technology. Pepecash has empowered artists to monetize their work, provided a platform for the tokenization of digital art, and created opportunities for artists and collectors to engage in a vibrant marketplace.

Pepecash's impact on the crypto art community extends beyond its technical functionalities. It has fostered a sense of community, collaboration, and innovation. Artists and collectors have come together to create unique Pepe-themed digital collectibles, participate in auctions and contests, and explore new ways of showcasing their creativity. Pepecash has facilitated a decentralized ecosystem where artists have direct access to their audience and can receive direct support for their work.

The fusion of art and technology enabled by Pepecash has also challenged traditional art market dynamics. With the transparency and immutability of blockchain technology, issues of provenance and ownership can be addressed more effectively. Pepecash has introduced a new paradigm for valuing and trading digital art, creating opportunities for artists to establish their market presence and establish their own economic models.

While Pepecash has experienced success and recognition within the crypto art community, it also faces challenges and uncertainties. The market for Pepe-themed digital collectibles is still relatively nascent, and sustainability is a key concern. Copyright issues and the need for continued innovation and development within the Pepecash ecosystem are factors that require careful attention.

Looking to the future, Pepecash has the potential to continue shaping the crypto art landscape. As blockchain technology evolves and adoption grows, Pepecash can explore new avenues for collaboration, expand its reach to a wider audience, and become a significant force within the broader art world. The intersection of art, technology, and decentralized finance has immense possibilities, and Pepecash's journey serves as an important case study in this evolving space.

In conclusion, Pepecash has emerged as a catalyst for change within the crypto art community. Through its empowering features, facilitation of tokenization, creation and trading of digital collectibles, and cultivation of collaborative projects and communities, Pepecash has left an indelible mark on the intersection of art and blockchain technology. Understanding its role provides valuable insights into the transformative potential of crypto art and the possibilities for artists and collectors in the digital age.

Chapter 3: Coinye, Scrypt, launched in 2014, USD 2 million ATH in Jan 2014
Background and history of Coinye

Introduction: Coinye, often referred to as "Coinye West," gained significant attention in the cryptocurrency world for its unique association with the popular American rapper Kanye West. In this section, we will delve into the background and history of Coinye, exploring its origins, development, and the factors that contributed to its rise and eventual downfall. Understanding the story of Coinye provides insights into the intersection of popular culture and cryptocurrency and the challenges faced by meme coins in the volatile crypto market.

1. The Genesis of Coinye: The story of Coinye begins with its early inception and the factors that led to its creation. We will explore the motivations behind the development of Coinye, including its association with Kanye West and the desire to create a cryptocurrency that would capture the attention of both cryptocurrency enthusiasts and fans of the rapper. This section will examine the early vision, goals, and aspirations of the Coinye project.

2. Coinye's Development and Features: We will delve into the technical aspects of Coinye, including its underlying Scrypt algorithm and the specific features that set it apart from other cryptocurrencies. This section will cover Coinye's blockchain technology, mining process, transaction verification, and its unique branding elements that incorporated Kanye West's image and persona. We will also discuss the considerations and challenges faced during the development phase of Coinye.

3. Launch and Initial Success: Coinye's launch in 2014 was met with significant media attention and early investor

interest. We will explore the events surrounding Coinye's launch, including the marketing strategies employed, the initial trading activity, and the community response. This section will also highlight Coinye's all-time high (ATH) value in January 2014, reaching a market capitalization of USD 2 million.

4. Legal Issues and Controversies: Coinye's journey was marred by legal issues and controversies, leading to its eventual demise. We will examine the legal challenges faced by Coinye, including trademark infringement allegations from Kanye West's legal team and the subsequent rebranding attempts. This section will also explore the role of intellectual property rights in the cryptocurrency landscape and the impact of legal actions on meme coins.

5. Community and Social Impact: Coinye's community played a significant role in its development and growth. We will analyze the dynamics of the Coinye community, including its online forums, social media presence, and collaborative initiatives. This section will also discuss the broader social impact of Coinye, including its role in raising awareness about cryptocurrencies and attracting new users to the crypto space.

6. Demise and Lessons Learned: Coinye's journey came to an abrupt end due to the legal battles and controversies it faced. We will analyze the factors that contributed to Coinye's downfall, including the regulatory challenges, loss of community support, and the overall volatility of the cryptocurrency market. This section will provide insights into the risks associated with meme coins and the importance of legal compliance and community engagement.

Conclusion: The story of Coinye represents a unique chapter in the history of meme coins and their association with popular culture. From its origins as a cryptocurrency inspired by Kanye West to its eventual demise due to legal challenges, Coinye's journey highlights the complexities and challenges faced by meme coins in the crypto market. Understanding the background and history of Coinye provides valuable insights into the intersection of popular culture and cryptocurrency, shedding light on the risks and opportunities that emerge in this volatile landscape.

Technical features of Scrypt

Introduction: Scrypt is a cryptographic algorithm that played a significant role in the development of Coinye and many other cryptocurrencies. In this section, we will explore the technical features of Scrypt, its advantages over other cryptographic algorithms, and its specific implementation within the Coinye blockchain. Understanding the technical aspects of Scrypt provides insights into the security, efficiency, and scalability of Coinye and its impact on the broader cryptocurrency landscape.

1. Introduction to Scrypt: We will begin by providing an overview of Scrypt as a cryptographic algorithm. This section will cover the fundamental principles behind Scrypt, its origins, and its intended purposes. We will discuss its key components, such as key derivation functions, password-based encryption, and the computational complexity that sets it apart from other algorithms.

2. Advantages of Scrypt: Scrypt offers several advantages over other cryptographic algorithms, and this section will explore these benefits in detail. We will discuss how Scrypt is designed to resist the computational power of specialized hardware (ASICs), making it more accessible to a broader range of users and promoting decentralization. We will also examine Scrypt's memory-hardness properties, which enhance the security of the network and make it resistant to certain types of attacks.

3. Scrypt in the Coinye Blockchain: Coinye utilized the Scrypt algorithm as its hashing function within its blockchain. We will explore the specific implementation of Scrypt within the Coinye network, including the hashing process, block generation, and transaction validation. This

section will also discuss how Scrypt contributes to the overall security and integrity of the Coinye blockchain.

4. Efficiency and Scalability Considerations: Scrypt's technical features have implications for the efficiency and scalability of the Coinye network. We will analyze how Scrypt's memory-intensive properties impact the computational requirements for mining and transaction processing. We will discuss the trade-offs between efficiency and security, as well as the challenges that arise as the network scales in terms of transaction volume and user activity.

5. Comparison with Other Cryptographic Algorithms: Scrypt is just one of many cryptographic algorithms used in the cryptocurrency space. In this section, we will compare Scrypt with other popular algorithms such as SHA-256 and Ethash. We will examine the strengths and weaknesses of each algorithm and discuss why Scrypt was chosen for Coinye and its specific use cases.

6. Future Developments and Challenges: Like any cryptographic algorithm, Scrypt is subject to ongoing research and development. This section will highlight the current advancements and potential future developments in Scrypt, including improvements in performance, security enhancements, and optimization techniques. We will also discuss the challenges and considerations for integrating these future developments into the Coinye network.

Conclusion: Scrypt is a fundamental component of the Coinye cryptocurrency, providing the underlying cryptographic security and hashing functions. Understanding the technical features of Scrypt allows us to appreciate its role in the Coinye ecosystem, its advantages over other algorithms, and its implications for network security, efficiency, and scalability. By examining Scrypt in the context of Coinye, we gain insights into the broader application of cryptographic algorithms in the cryptocurrency landscape and their impact on the development and functionality of digital currencies.

Introduction: The launch of Coinye in 2014 marked an important milestone in the world of cryptocurrencies. In this section, we will delve into the background and details surrounding the launch of Coinye, including the motivation behind its creation, the development process, the community involvement, and the initial reception by the cryptocurrency community. Understanding the launch of Coinye provides insights into the factors that contributed to its rise in popularity and its subsequent challenges.

1. Genesis of Coinye: The story of Coinye's launch begins with its genesis. We will explore the origins of Coinye, including the individuals or group behind its creation and their inspiration. We will delve into the initial vision for Coinye and the goals the developers sought to achieve in the cryptocurrency space. Understanding the genesis of Coinye is essential to comprehend the context in which it was launched and the motivations behind its unique branding and identity.

2. Development and Technical Implementation: The successful launch of any cryptocurrency requires meticulous planning and technical expertise. This section will delve into the development process of Coinye, including the choice of the Scrypt algorithm, the design of the blockchain, the implementation of mining protocols, and the creation of the wallet software. We will explore the technical challenges encountered during the development phase and the strategies employed to overcome them.

3. Community Involvement and Initial Reception: The success of a cryptocurrency heavily relies on community engagement and adoption. We will examine the role of the Coinye community during its launch, including the early

adopters, enthusiasts, and miners who contributed to the network's growth. We will discuss the initial reception of Coinye within the cryptocurrency community, analyzing the factors that attracted users and the unique marketing strategies employed to promote its adoption.

4. Branding and Legal Challenges: Coinye's launch was accompanied by unique branding and association with popular culture figures. This section will explore the legal challenges faced by Coinye due to its branding, including the cease-and-desist letters received from celebrities. We will analyze the impact of these legal battles on the project's trajectory, community sentiment, and long-term sustainability.

5. Market Performance and Price Analysis: Examining the market performance of Coinye provides valuable insights into its initial success and subsequent challenges. We will analyze the price history of Coinye, including its all-time high (ATH) in January 2014, and the factors that contributed to its price volatility. We will discuss the role of speculative trading, investor sentiment, and external market factors in shaping Coinye's market performance during its early days.

6. Lessons Learned and Legacy: The launch of Coinye, despite its eventual challenges and legal issues, left a lasting impact on the cryptocurrency community. In this section, we will reflect on the lessons learned from the launch of Coinye, the potential pitfalls to avoid, and the opportunities that emerged from this unique experience. We will discuss the legacy of Coinye and its influence on subsequent meme coins and cryptocurrency projects.

Conclusion: The launch of Coinye in 2014 showcased the power of community engagement, unique branding, and innovative marketing strategies in the cryptocurrency world.

By examining the background, development process, community involvement, legal challenges, market performance, and lessons learned, we gain a comprehensive understanding of the launch of Coinye and its impact on the broader cryptocurrency landscape. Coinye's story serves as a valuable case study for aspiring cryptocurrency projects and highlights the importance of careful planning, community building, and legal compliance in the early stages of a cryptocurrency's existence.

Market performance of Coinye

Introduction: The market performance of a cryptocurrency is a crucial aspect that determines its success and acceptance within the broader cryptocurrency ecosystem. In this section, we will explore the market performance of Coinye, analyzing its price history, market capitalization, trading volume, and overall market sentiment. By examining these factors, we can gain insights into the factors that influenced Coinye's market performance and its subsequent trajectory.

1. Initial Price Movement: The early days of Coinye were characterized by significant price volatility. We will delve into the initial price movement of Coinye, examining its launch price, subsequent price spikes, and the factors that contributed to these price fluctuations. We will analyze the role of market speculation, early adopters, and trading activity in shaping Coinye's price trajectory during its early stages.

2. Factors Influencing Market Sentiment: Understanding the factors that influenced market sentiment is crucial to comprehending Coinye's market performance. We will explore the role of external factors, such as media coverage, celebrity endorsements, and the broader cryptocurrency market trends, in shaping investor perception and sentiment towards Coinye. Additionally, we will analyze the impact of community engagement, social media discussions, and online forums on the overall market sentiment surrounding Coinye.

3. Trading Volume and Liquidity: Trading volume and liquidity are essential metrics for evaluating the market performance of a cryptocurrency. We will assess the trading volume of Coinye across different exchanges, analyzing the

patterns of buying and selling activity. By examining the liquidity of Coinye, we can gain insights into its market depth and the ease with which investors could buy or sell the cryptocurrency.

4. Market Capitalization and Ranking: Market capitalization serves as a key indicator of a cryptocurrency's overall value and market position. We will analyze Coinye's market capitalization over time, tracking its ranking relative to other cryptocurrencies. By understanding Coinye's market capitalization and ranking, we can assess its level of adoption and investor interest within the broader cryptocurrency market.

5. Community Engagement and Investor Sentiment: The role of the community and investor sentiment cannot be overlooked when evaluating the market performance of Coinye. We will examine the level of community engagement, including the size of the Coinye community, online discussions, and community-driven initiatives. We will also analyze investor sentiment towards Coinye, including sentiment analysis from social media platforms and investor surveys, to gain insights into the perception and sentiment surrounding the cryptocurrency.

6. Long-Term Sustainability: Assessing the long-term sustainability of Coinye's market performance is crucial to understanding its overall trajectory. We will examine the challenges and obstacles faced by Coinye, including the legal battles and controversies surrounding its branding, and their impact on its market performance. Additionally, we will discuss the potential factors that contributed to Coinye's decline in market value and its long-term sustainability as a cryptocurrency project.

Conclusion: The market performance of Coinye played a significant role in shaping its trajectory and overall acceptance within the cryptocurrency community. By analyzing its price movements, market capitalization, trading volume, community engagement, and investor sentiment, we gain valuable insights into the factors that influenced Coinye's market performance. Coinye's story serves as a reminder of the importance of market dynamics, community engagement, and external factors in the success or failure of a cryptocurrency. Understanding Coinye's market performance provides valuable lessons for investors, enthusiasts, and aspiring cryptocurrency projects in navigating the dynamic cryptocurrency market.

Introduction: The cryptocurrency industry has often been associated with legal challenges and controversies, and Coinye was no exception. In this section, we will delve into the legal issues and controversies surrounding Coinye, examining the factors that led to its legal battles, trademark disputes, and eventual downfall. By analyzing these events, we can gain insights into the legal complexities and regulatory hurdles faced by cryptocurrencies and their impact on Coinye's trajectory.

1. Trademark Disputes: Coinye faced significant legal challenges related to trademark disputes. We will explore the origins of these disputes, examining the conflicts that arose between the Coinye development team and notable individuals or entities. We will analyze the claims made by trademark holders and their efforts to protect their intellectual property rights, which resulted in legal battles and ultimately affected Coinye's ability to operate under its original branding.

2. Regulatory Compliance: Regulatory compliance is a crucial aspect of any cryptocurrency project. We will discuss the regulatory landscape during Coinye's launch and subsequent operation, including the challenges it faced in adhering to regulatory requirements. We will analyze the role of government agencies and regulatory bodies in monitoring and enforcing compliance, and the impact of regulatory actions on Coinye's operations and market performance.

3. Shutdown and Rebranding: Due to the legal battles and trademark disputes, Coinye faced significant challenges in maintaining its operations under its original branding. We will examine the circumstances that led to the shutdown of

Coinye's original project and the subsequent rebranding efforts. We will discuss the motivations behind the rebranding and the impact it had on Coinye's overall trajectory.

4. Intellectual Property Rights: The issue of intellectual property rights played a central role in the legal controversies surrounding Coinye. We will explore the complexities of intellectual property laws and their application to cryptocurrency projects. We will analyze the arguments put forth by both Coinye and the trademark holders, and the legal interpretations of intellectual property rights in the context of digital assets and blockchain technology.

5. Lessons Learned: The legal issues and controversies surrounding Coinye provide valuable lessons for the cryptocurrency community. We will discuss the implications of these legal battles for other cryptocurrency projects, including the importance of intellectual property rights, the need for regulatory compliance, and the potential risks associated with trademark disputes. We will examine the impact of these events on the broader cryptocurrency industry and the subsequent efforts made by other projects to navigate legal challenges.

6. Future Outlook: Looking ahead, we will discuss the potential implications of the legal issues and controversies surrounding Coinye for the future of cryptocurrency projects. We will explore the evolving regulatory landscape and the steps taken by the industry to address legal challenges and ensure compliance. We will also discuss the role of intellectual property rights in the cryptocurrency ecosystem and the potential impact on innovation and development.

Conclusion: The legal issues and controversies surrounding Coinye highlight the complexities and challenges faced by cryptocurrency projects in navigating the legal landscape. Coinye's trademark disputes, regulatory compliance challenges, and eventual shutdown serve as important case studies for the cryptocurrency community. By understanding the legal issues surrounding Coinye, we can learn valuable lessons about intellectual property rights, regulatory compliance, and the potential risks and hurdles faced by cryptocurrency projects. These insights are crucial for the industry as it continues to evolve and seeks wider adoption in the face of legal complexities.

Chapter 4: 42 Coin, Scrypt, launched in 2014, USD 1.2 million ATH in Jan 2014

Background and history of 42 Coin

Introduction: In this chapter, we will explore the background and history of 42 Coin, a unique cryptocurrency that captured the attention of the crypto community with its limited supply and high market value. We will delve into the origins of 42 Coin, its development team, and the factors that contributed to its creation. By understanding the background and history of 42 Coin, we can gain insights into its unique characteristics and the reasons behind its success in the early days of the cryptocurrency market.

1. Genesis and Inspiration: To understand the background of 42 Coin, we need to explore its genesis and the inspiration behind its creation. We will delve into the motivations of the developers and the ideas that shaped the concept of 42 Coin. We will also examine the significance of the number 42 in popular culture and its connection to the cryptocurrency's name and branding.

2. Development Team and Community: The success of any cryptocurrency project depends on the individuals involved in its development and the community that supports it. We will explore the background of the 42 Coin development team, their expertise, and their contributions to the project. Additionally, we will examine the community that formed around 42 Coin, including early adopters, enthusiasts, and contributors who helped shape its trajectory.

3. Technical Features of 42 Coin: To comprehend the uniqueness of 42 Coin, we need to delve into its technical features. We will discuss the underlying technology behind 42 Coin, including its utilization of the Scrypt algorithm. We

will explore the technical specifications, such as block time, block rewards, and mining difficulty, that differentiate 42 Coin from other cryptocurrencies. Furthermore, we will examine the rationale behind these technical choices and their impact on the coin's value and scarcity.

4. Launch and Distribution: The launch and distribution of 42 Coin played a crucial role in its early adoption and market performance. We will explore the timeline leading up to the launch, the methods of distribution, and the initial response from the crypto community. We will analyze the factors that contributed to the coin's initial success and the strategies employed to create scarcity and value.

5. Market Performance and Price History: One of the defining aspects of 42 Coin is its remarkable market performance and price history. We will examine the coin's price movements, market capitalization, and trading volume over time. We will discuss the factors that influenced the coin's value, including demand, scarcity, market sentiment, and external events. Additionally, we will analyze the factors that contributed to its all-time high in January 2014.

6. Use Cases and Adoption: Beyond its market value, we will explore the use cases and adoption of 42 Coin. We will discuss the industries and communities that embraced 42 Coin as a means of exchange or store of value. We will also examine the challenges and opportunities for adoption faced by 42 Coin and its potential impact on the wider cryptocurrency ecosystem.

Conclusion: The background and history of 42 Coin provide valuable insights into the unique characteristics and early success of this cryptocurrency. By understanding its genesis, development team, technical features, launch, market performance, and use cases, we can appreciate the factors that contributed to its popularity and market value. The story of 42 Coin serves as an important case study in the cryptocurrency landscape, demonstrating how a combination of scarcity, technical innovation, and community support can shape the trajectory of a cryptocurrency project.

Technical features of Scrypt

Introduction: In this chapter, we will explore the technical features of Scrypt, the algorithm used by 42 Coin. Understanding the technical aspects of Scrypt is crucial for comprehending the underlying infrastructure and functionality of 42 Coin. We will delve into the characteristics of Scrypt, its advantages over other algorithms, and its role in maintaining the security and integrity of the 42 Coin network. By examining the technical features of Scrypt, readers will gain a comprehensive understanding of the technological foundations that enable the existence and operation of 42 Coin.

1. Overview of Scrypt: To begin our exploration of Scrypt, we will provide an overview of the algorithm and its purpose within the cryptocurrency ecosystem. We will explain the key concepts and components of Scrypt, including its cryptographic functions, memory-intensive properties, and resistance to specialized mining hardware. Additionally, we will discuss the motivation behind the development of Scrypt and its evolution over time.

2. Security and Integrity: One of the fundamental aspects of any cryptographic algorithm is its ability to ensure the security and integrity of the network. We will analyze how Scrypt achieves these objectives through its use of cryptographic primitives and techniques. We will discuss the mechanisms employed by Scrypt to protect against attacks, such as brute-force attacks and cryptographic vulnerabilities. Furthermore, we will explore the role of Scrypt in mitigating the risks associated with mining centralization and 51% attacks.

3. Memory Requirements and Efficiency: Scrypt is known for its memory-intensive properties, which provide

resistance against specialized mining hardware and foster a more decentralized mining ecosystem. We will delve into the memory requirements of Scrypt and their impact on the mining process. We will discuss the advantages of memory-intensive algorithms in terms of energy consumption, mining accessibility, and network security. Additionally, we will explore the trade-offs and considerations associated with memory requirements in the context of Scrypt.

4. Mining and Consensus: Mining plays a crucial role in the operation of any cryptocurrency network. We will examine how Scrypt facilitates the mining process for 42 Coin, including the generation of new coins and the validation of transactions. We will discuss the consensus mechanism employed by Scrypt, exploring how it ensures the agreement and synchronization of the network participants. Furthermore, we will analyze the mining ecosystem surrounding Scrypt-based cryptocurrencies, including mining pools, hardware requirements, and the distribution of mining rewards.

5. Scalability and Future Developments: As cryptocurrencies continue to evolve, scalability becomes an important consideration. We will discuss the scalability challenges associated with Scrypt and explore the ongoing developments and research efforts aimed at addressing these challenges. We will examine potential solutions, such as layer-two protocols and off-chain scaling, and their applicability to Scrypt-based cryptocurrencies. Additionally, we will explore the future developments and enhancements that could further improve the scalability and performance of Scrypt.

Conclusion: Understanding the technical features of Scrypt is essential for comprehending the underlying infrastructure and functionality of 42 Coin. By examining the characteristics of Scrypt, including its security and integrity, memory requirements and efficiency, mining and consensus mechanisms, scalability challenges, and future developments, readers gain a comprehensive understanding of the technological foundations that enable the existence and operation of 42 Coin. The technical aspects of Scrypt highlight the innovation and complexity behind 42 Coin, contributing to its uniqueness and appeal within the cryptocurrency ecosystem.

Launch of 42 Coin in 2014

Introduction: In this chapter, we will delve into the launch of 42 Coin, a cryptocurrency based on the Scrypt algorithm. The launch of a cryptocurrency is a significant event that marks the beginning of its journey and sets the stage for its adoption and growth. We will explore the background and history leading up to the launch of 42 Coin, the key players involved, the motivations behind its creation, and the strategies employed to introduce it to the cryptocurrency community. By understanding the launch of 42 Coin, readers will gain insights into the factors that contributed to its initial success and the challenges it faced in its early stages.

1. Genesis of 42 Coin: To understand the launch of 42 Coin, it is essential to examine the genesis of the project. We will explore the motivations and ideas that inspired the creation of 42 Coin, including the vision for a unique and exclusive cryptocurrency. We will delve into the origins of the project, the individuals or group behind it, and the objectives they aimed to achieve through the development of 42 Coin. By understanding the genesis of 42 Coin, we can gain insights into its intended purpose and the values it sought to embody.

2. Development and Preparation: The successful launch of a cryptocurrency requires careful planning, development, and preparation. We will explore the technical aspects of developing 42 Coin, including the programming languages, tools, and frameworks used in its creation. We will also discuss the steps taken to ensure the stability, security, and functionality of the network, such as testing, code reviews, and audits. Additionally, we will examine the preparations made to promote and introduce 42 Coin to the

cryptocurrency community, including marketing strategies, community engagement, and partnerships.

3. Initial Distribution and Mining: The distribution of a cryptocurrency's initial supply is a crucial aspect of its launch. We will discuss how the creators of 42 Coin approached the initial distribution process and the mechanisms employed to ensure fairness and inclusivity. We will explore the mining process for 42 Coin, including the hardware requirements, mining algorithms, and rewards structure. Additionally, we will examine the role of mining pools, early adopters, and enthusiasts in the initial distribution and mining of 42 Coin.

4. Early Adoption and Community Building: Building a strong and engaged community is vital for the success of any cryptocurrency. We will analyze the strategies employed by the creators of 42 Coin to foster early adoption and community building. We will discuss the platforms and channels used to promote 42 Coin, the incentives provided to encourage participation and engagement, and the initiatives taken to attract developers, investors, and users. Furthermore, we will explore the challenges faced in building a community and how they were overcome.

5. Initial Market Performance: The launch of 42 Coin in 2014 was accompanied by its initial market performance. We will analyze the price dynamics, trading volume, and market sentiment surrounding 42 Coin during its early days. We will discuss the factors that influenced the market perception and valuation of 42 Coin, including the overall cryptocurrency market conditions, media coverage, and investor sentiment. Additionally, we will explore the challenges and opportunities that emerged from the initial market performance of 42 Coin.

Conclusion: The launch of 42 Coin in 2014 marked the beginning of its journey as a unique and exclusive cryptocurrency. By exploring the background and history leading up to its launch, the development and preparation process, the initial distribution and mining strategies, the efforts in building a community, and the early market performance, readers gain insights into the factors that contributed to its initial success and the challenges it faced. The launch of 42 Coin represents a significant milestone in the evolution of the cryptocurrency landscape. It showcased the innovative application of the Scrypt algorithm and demonstrated the potential for creating cryptocurrencies with limited supply and exclusivity. The meticulous development and preparation process ensured a robust and secure network, instilling confidence among early adopters and enthusiasts. The fair and inclusive initial distribution mechanism fostered a sense of community and encouraged widespread participation. The early market performance of 42 Coin reflected the growing interest in cryptocurrencies at the time, as evidenced by its valuation and trading volume. However, like any nascent cryptocurrency, it faced its fair share of challenges, including establishing liquidity, gaining wider adoption, and navigating the volatile and competitive market. Nevertheless, the launch of 42 Coin set the stage for its subsequent development and growth, paving the way for its unique community, use cases, and long-term potential.

Moving forward, it would be interesting to examine how 42 Coin has evolved since its launch, including its adaptation to changing market conditions, its integration with other platforms and services, and its impact on the broader cryptocurrency ecosystem. Additionally, analyzing the lessons learned from the launch of 42 Coin can provide valuable insights for future cryptocurrency projects, guiding their development, distribution, and community-building strategies.

Overall, the launch of 42 Coin in 2014 represents a significant chapter in the history of cryptocurrencies. It exemplifies the ingenuity and creativity of cryptocurrency developers and enthusiasts, showcasing their ability to create unique and exclusive digital assets. Understanding the background, technical features, and market performance of 42 Coin provides a holistic view of its journey, highlighting the opportunities and challenges faced by early cryptocurrencies in a rapidly evolving industry.

Introduction: The market performance of a cryptocurrency is a crucial aspect that reflects its acceptance, value, and overall success. In the case of 42 Coin, its unique characteristics and limited supply positioned it as an intriguing investment opportunity. This subtopic delves into the market performance of 42 Coin, analyzing its price movements, trading volume, market capitalization, investor sentiment, and the factors that influenced its performance.

1. Early Price Movements and Volatility: The initial stages of 42 Coin's market journey witnessed notable price movements and volatility. Examining the price history can provide insights into the demand and market sentiment surrounding the cryptocurrency. Factors such as scarcity, media attention, and market speculation may have contributed to fluctuations in its price. This section delves into the early price movements of 42 Coin, including its initial valuation, price discovery, and the factors influencing its volatility.

2. Factors Influencing Market Sentiment: Understanding the factors that influenced market sentiment towards 42 Coin is crucial in comprehending its market performance. Factors such as media coverage, community engagement, technological developments, regulatory environment, and market trends played a role in shaping investors' perception and confidence in the cryptocurrency. This section explores the various factors that impacted the market sentiment surrounding 42 Coin, highlighting their significance in shaping its performance.

3. Trading Volume and Liquidity: The trading volume and liquidity of a cryptocurrency are key indicators of its market activity and investor interest. This section focuses on

analyzing the trading volume of 42 Coin across different exchanges, liquidity dynamics, and the presence of market makers. Examining the trading patterns and liquidity can provide insights into the market depth and accessibility of 42 Coin, shedding light on its attractiveness to investors and traders.

4. Market Capitalization and Ranking: Market capitalization serves as a widely recognized metric for evaluating the size and value of a cryptocurrency. This section delves into the market capitalization of 42 Coin over time, comparing it with other cryptocurrencies and examining its ranking within the cryptocurrency market. Analyzing the market capitalization and ranking of 42 Coin provides a measure of its market acceptance and competitiveness.

5. Investor Sentiment and Community Engagement: The sentiment of investors and the level of community engagement are critical factors in determining the success of a cryptocurrency. This section explores the sentiment surrounding 42 Coin, including investor perception, sentiment analysis, and the role of community engagement in shaping the cryptocurrency's market performance. Examining the involvement and support of the community can provide insights into the long-term sustainability and growth potential of 42 Coin.

6. Impact of External Factors: The market performance of 42 Coin was influenced by external factors beyond its inherent characteristics. This section examines the impact of broader market trends, regulatory developments, technological advancements, and economic factors on the performance of 42 Coin. Understanding the

interplay between 42 Coin and the external environment provides a comprehensive view of its market performance.

Conclusion: The market performance of 42 Coin played a significant role in establishing its position within the cryptocurrency ecosystem. Analyzing its early price movements, factors influencing market sentiment, trading volume, market capitalization, investor sentiment, and community engagement provides valuable insights into its acceptance and value. The market performance of 42 Coin reflected both the opportunities and challenges faced by a unique cryptocurrency in a dynamic and competitive market. Understanding its market performance contributes to a comprehensive understanding of 42 Coin's journey and its impact on the broader cryptocurrency landscape.

Community and use cases of 42 Coin

Introduction: The success of a cryptocurrency often relies on the strength and engagement of its community. In the case of 42 Coin, its unique attributes and limited supply attracted a specific community of users. This subtopic explores the community surrounding 42 Coin, their involvement, use cases, and the impact they have on the cryptocurrency's ecosystem. Additionally, it examines the practical applications and real-world use cases of 42 Coin, shedding light on its value proposition beyond being a digital asset.

1. Formation and Growth of the 42 Coin Community: The community surrounding 42 Coin played a crucial role in shaping its development and success. This section explores the formation of the 42 Coin community, its early adopters, and the initiatives undertaken to foster engagement. It delves into the channels of communication, community governance, and the collaborative efforts to promote the adoption and utilization of 42 Coin.

2. Engagement and Participation: The level of engagement and participation within the 42 Coin community is a reflection of its vibrancy and strength. This section examines the various forms of engagement, including online forums, social media platforms, and dedicated community channels. It explores the participation of community members in discussions, knowledge sharing, support, and the promotion of 42 Coin within the broader cryptocurrency community.

3. Use Cases and Practical Applications: Beyond being a digital asset, 42 Coin has sought to establish itself with practical use cases and applications. This section explores the different ways in which 42 Coin can be utilized and the

industries or sectors that can benefit from its unique features. It examines potential use cases such as e-commerce, remittances, micropayments, decentralized applications, and store-of-value. Additionally, it delves into partnerships or collaborations that enhance the adoption and integration of 42 Coin in real-world scenarios.

4. Community-driven Projects and Initiatives: The 42 Coin community has been instrumental in driving projects and initiatives that showcase its utility and innovation. This section highlights community-driven projects, such as the development of applications, platforms, or services that leverage the capabilities of 42 Coin. It explores the entrepreneurial spirit within the community and the collaborative efforts to expand the reach and impact of 42 Coin in different domains.

5. Education and Awareness: Educating the community and raising awareness about the benefits and potential of 42 Coin is crucial for its long-term growth and sustainability. This section delves into educational initiatives undertaken by the community, including tutorials, articles, webinars, and educational materials. It also explores the efforts made to raise awareness about 42 Coin through marketing campaigns, events, and partnerships.

6. Community Governance and Decision-making: Community governance plays a vital role in shaping the trajectory of a cryptocurrency. This section examines the governance model and decision-making processes within the 42 Coin community. It explores mechanisms such as voting systems, consensus-building, and community proposals. Understanding the governance structure and community-driven decision-making provides insights into the democratic nature and sustainability of 42 Coin.

Conclusion: The community surrounding 42 Coin has been instrumental in its growth, adoption, and the development of practical use cases. Analyzing the formation and growth of the community, their engagement and participation, as well as the practical applications and real-world use cases, sheds light on the broader impact of 42 Coin beyond being a digital asset. The community-driven projects, educational initiatives, and governance mechanisms demonstrate the vibrancy and collaborative nature of the 42 Coin ecosystem. Understanding the community and use cases of 42 Coin provides valuable insights into its potential as a digital currency and its role within the broader cryptocurrency landscape.

Chapter 5: FedoraCoin, Scrypt, launched in 2014, USD 0.5 million ATH in Jan 2014

Background and history of FedoraCoin

Introduction: FedoraCoin, also known as TIPS (TiPS), is a unique cryptocurrency that gained attention for its community-centric approach and philanthropic initiatives. This subtopic delves into the background and history of FedoraCoin, exploring its origins, development, key milestones, and the driving forces behind its creation. By understanding the foundation on which FedoraCoin was built, readers can gain insights into its unique characteristics and the factors that shaped its evolution.

1. Origins of FedoraCoin: The origins of FedoraCoin trace back to the early days of cryptocurrency development. This section explores the motivations and vision of the creators behind FedoraCoin, the inspiration they drew from existing cryptocurrencies, and the unique aspects they sought to introduce. It delves into the technological innovations and community-driven philosophy that formed the basis of FedoraCoin's creation.

2. Development and Early Milestones: The development process of FedoraCoin involved a dedicated team of developers and community contributors. This section highlights the key milestones in the early stages of FedoraCoin, including the launch of the network, the development of the blockchain, and the introduction of important features. It also examines the challenges faced during the development process and the strategies employed to overcome them.

3. Community Engagement and Philanthropic Initiatives: FedoraCoin differentiated itself from other cryptocurrencies by placing a strong emphasis on

community engagement and philanthropy. This section explores the ways in which the FedoraCoin community was fostered, including online forums, social media channels, and dedicated community events. It also highlights the various philanthropic initiatives undertaken by the FedoraCoin community, such as donations to charitable causes and supporting projects that align with the community's values.

4. Technological Features and Innovations: FedoraCoin introduced several technological features and innovations that set it apart from other cryptocurrencies. This section explores the technical aspects of FedoraCoin, including its use of the Scrypt algorithm, the consensus mechanism, and the technical infrastructure that supports its functionality. It also examines any unique features or enhancements introduced by FedoraCoin that contributed to its popularity and adoption.

5. Partnerships and Collaborations: Collaborations and partnerships played a significant role in shaping the trajectory of FedoraCoin. This section explores the collaborations with businesses, organizations, and other cryptocurrencies that helped to expand the reach and use cases of FedoraCoin. It examines the synergies created through these partnerships and the mutual benefits derived from such collaborations.

6. Evolution and Adaptation: The evolution of FedoraCoin over time reflects its ability to adapt to changing market conditions and technological advancements. This section examines the updates, improvements, and upgrades made to FedoraCoin's protocol, wallet software, and infrastructure. It also explores how FedoraCoin responded to

challenges and market trends, ensuring its relevance and longevity in the cryptocurrency ecosystem.

Conclusion: The background and history of FedoraCoin provide valuable insights into its origins, development, and unique characteristics. By understanding the motivations of its creators, the community-centric approach, and the philanthropic initiatives, readers can appreciate the underlying values that shape FedoraCoin's ecosystem. The technological features, partnerships, and adaptations demonstrate FedoraCoin's ability to evolve and remain relevant in a rapidly changing cryptocurrency landscape. Examining the background and history of FedoraCoin sets the stage for a deeper exploration of its market performance, community engagement, and potential use cases, which further enhances our understanding of its significance within the broader cryptocurrency ecosystem.

Introduction: Scrypt is the cryptographic algorithm employed by FedoraCoin (TIPS) and several other cryptocurrencies. It was designed to address the limitations of Bitcoin's SHA-256 algorithm and provide enhanced security and performance for mining and transaction processing. This subtopic explores the technical features of Scrypt, its underlying principles, and its impact on the functionality and operation of FedoraCoin.

1. Overview of Scrypt: This section provides an overview of the Scrypt algorithm, explaining its purpose and distinguishing characteristics. It examines how Scrypt differs from other cryptographic algorithms, such as SHA-256, and outlines the key components and processes involved in Scrypt's operation. Additionally, it discusses the rationale behind selecting Scrypt as the hashing algorithm for FedoraCoin.

2. Key Components of Scrypt: To understand Scrypt's technical features, it is essential to delve into its key components. This section explores the building blocks of Scrypt, including its use of random access memory (RAM), the concept of the Salsa20/8 core, and the PBKDF2 (Password-Based Key Derivation Function 2) key stretching algorithm. It explains how these components work together to ensure the security and efficiency of the Scrypt algorithm.

3. Security Enhancements: Scrypt was specifically designed to address certain vulnerabilities associated with Bitcoin's SHA-256 algorithm. This section examines the security enhancements offered by Scrypt, including its resistance to ASIC (Application-Specific Integrated Circuit) mining, its reliance on memory-hard computations, and its protection against brute-force attacks. It also discusses the

concept of key stretching and its role in strengthening security within Scrypt.

4. Performance Considerations: Scrypt's performance characteristics have a significant impact on the mining process, transaction verification, and overall network efficiency. This section explores the performance considerations associated with Scrypt, including its memory requirements, computational complexity, and energy efficiency. It also discusses the implications of Scrypt's performance on the scalability and transaction processing speed of FedoraCoin.

5. Comparative Analysis: To better understand Scrypt's technical features, it is valuable to compare it with other cryptographic algorithms. This section provides a comparative analysis of Scrypt and SHA-256, highlighting the advantages and disadvantages of each algorithm. It explores the computational requirements, memory usage, and potential vulnerabilities associated with both algorithms, allowing readers to gain insights into Scrypt's unique attributes.

6. Future Developments and Adaptations: Like any technology, Scrypt continues to evolve over time. This section explores the ongoing developments and adaptations in the field of Scrypt, including optimizations, updates, and potential enhancements. It discusses the research and advancements aimed at improving Scrypt's efficiency, security, and usability, and their potential impact on the future of FedoraCoin and other cryptocurrencies utilizing Scrypt.

Conclusion: The technical features of Scrypt play a crucial role in shaping the functionality and operation of FedoraCoin. By understanding the underlying principles of

Scrypt, its security enhancements, performance considerations, and ongoing developments, readers can appreciate the technical foundation on which FedoraCoin is built. Scrypt's memory-hard computations, resistance to ASIC mining, and key stretching algorithms contribute to the security and decentralization of FedoraCoin's network. Evaluating the technical features of Scrypt enhances our understanding of FedoraCoin's capabilities, its positioning within the cryptocurrency landscape, and its potential for future growth and adoption.

Launch of FedoraCoin in 2014

Introduction: The launch of FedoraCoin (TIPS) in 2014 marked a significant milestone in the history of cryptocurrencies. This subtopic explores the background and history leading up to the launch of FedoraCoin, the motivations behind its creation, the technical aspects of the launch, and the initial distribution and adoption strategies employed. By examining the launch of FedoraCoin, readers gain insights into its early development, the community's response, and the challenges faced by the project.

1. Motivations and Conceptualization: To understand the launch of FedoraCoin, it is essential to explore the motivations and conceptualization behind its creation. This section delves into the vision and goals of the project's founders, their inspiration for developing a new cryptocurrency, and their aspirations for FedoraCoin within the broader crypto ecosystem. It discusses the driving factors that led to the conceptualization of FedoraCoin and its unique features.

2. Technical Preparation and Development: The successful launch of a cryptocurrency requires meticulous technical preparation and development. This section examines the technical aspects involved in preparing for the launch of FedoraCoin. It explores the selection and customization of the Scrypt algorithm, the development of the blockchain infrastructure, the creation of the FedoraCoin wallet, and the testing and debugging processes. It highlights the challenges faced and overcome during the technical development phase.

3. Initial Coin Offering (ICO) and Token Distribution: The launch of FedoraCoin involved the distribution of its native tokens to early adopters and supporters. This section

explores the initial coin offering (ICO) or token sale process used to distribute FedoraCoin tokens. It discusses the strategies employed to attract participants, the allocation and distribution methods, and the transparency and fairness considerations. Additionally, it examines the response from the crypto community and the level of participation during the token distribution phase.

4. Community Building and Adoption Strategies: The success of any cryptocurrency project depends heavily on community engagement and adoption. This section explores the community building and adoption strategies employed during the launch of FedoraCoin. It discusses the efforts to attract developers, miners, and users to the ecosystem, the establishment of online communities and forums, and the promotion of FedoraCoin through social media and other channels. It also examines the partnerships and collaborations that contributed to the initial adoption of FedoraCoin.

5. Challenges and Lessons Learned: The launch of FedoraCoin was not without its challenges. This section discusses the obstacles and setbacks encountered during the launch phase and the lessons learned from those experiences. It explores technical issues, regulatory compliance considerations, market volatility, and community management challenges. By understanding the challenges faced by the FedoraCoin project, readers gain insights into the complexities and risks involved in launching a cryptocurrency.

6. Impact and Legacy: The launch of FedoraCoin had a lasting impact on the cryptocurrency landscape. This section examines the legacy of FedoraCoin and its contributions to the broader crypto community. It explores

the innovations and unique features introduced by FedoraCoin, its influence on subsequent projects, and the lessons learned from its launch. Additionally, it discusses the continued development and evolution of FedoraCoin after its initial launch.

Conclusion: The launch of FedoraCoin in 2014 was a crucial moment in its history, marking the beginning of its journey as a unique and innovative cryptocurrency. By examining the motivations behind its creation, the technical preparation and development, the ICO and token distribution process, the community building and adoption strategies, the challenges faced, and the project's impact and legacy, readers gain a comprehensive understanding of the launch of FedoraCoin. This knowledge provides insights into the early days of FedoraCoin's development, its positioning within the crypto ecosystem, and its potential for future growth and adoption.

Introduction: The market performance of FedoraCoin (TIPS) plays a crucial role in assessing its reception, adoption, and overall success within the cryptocurrency ecosystem. This subtopic explores the price dynamics, trading volume, market capitalization, and investor sentiment surrounding FedoraCoin. By analyzing the market performance, readers gain insights into the factors that influenced FedoraCoin's valuation, its position among other cryptocurrencies, and the challenges it faced in maintaining market stability and growth.

1. Initial Price Discovery: The initial stages of FedoraCoin's market performance were marked by price discovery and volatility. This section examines the early price movements, including the initial listing on cryptocurrency exchanges, the factors influencing price discovery, and the market sentiment during this period. It explores the fluctuations and the impact of supply and demand dynamics on the price of FedoraCoin.

2. Trading Volume and Liquidity: Trading volume and liquidity are crucial indicators of a cryptocurrency's market performance. This section analyzes the trading volume of FedoraCoin and its liquidity across various exchanges. It discusses the factors that influenced trading activity, such as news events, partnerships, and community engagement. It also explores the liquidity challenges faced by FedoraCoin and the efforts made to improve market liquidity.

3. Market Capitalization and Ranking: Market capitalization provides a measure of a cryptocurrency's value and market position. This section examines the market capitalization of FedoraCoin and its ranking among other cryptocurrencies during different phases of its market

performance. It discusses the factors that contributed to fluctuations in market capitalization and the significance of ranking within the broader crypto market.

4. Investor Sentiment and Community Engagement: Investor sentiment and community engagement are vital factors in determining the market performance of a cryptocurrency. This section explores the sentiment of investors and the broader community towards FedoraCoin. It analyzes community engagement metrics such as social media activity, online forums, and developer contributions. It also discusses the impact of positive and negative news events on investor sentiment and the efforts made to foster a strong and supportive community.

5. Adoption and Use Cases: The market performance of FedoraCoin is closely tied to its adoption and use cases. This section examines the adoption of FedoraCoin as a means of payment and its integration into various platforms and services. It explores partnerships, merchant acceptance, and the development of applications utilizing FedoraCoin. Additionally, it discusses the challenges faced in achieving widespread adoption and the potential use cases that drove market interest.

6. Challenges and Price Stability: Maintaining price stability is a significant challenge for any cryptocurrency. This section discusses the challenges faced by FedoraCoin in maintaining a stable price and the measures taken to address price volatility. It explores the impact of external factors such as market trends, regulatory developments, and technological advancements on the price stability of FedoraCoin. It also examines the role of market manipulation and the steps taken to mitigate such activities.

Conclusion: The market performance of FedoraCoin reflects its reception and adoption within the cryptocurrency ecosystem. By analyzing the initial price discovery, trading volume, market capitalization, investor sentiment, community engagement, adoption, and challenges related to price stability, readers gain a comprehensive understanding of FedoraCoin's market performance. This knowledge provides insights into the factors that influenced FedoraCoin's valuation, its position among other cryptocurrencies, and its potential for future growth and sustainability.

Unique aspects of FedoraCoin compared to other cryptocurrencies

Introduction: FedoraCoin (TIPS) distinguishes itself from other cryptocurrencies through its unique features, functionality, and community-driven initiatives. This subtopic explores the distinctive aspects of FedoraCoin that set it apart from other digital currencies. By examining its innovative use cases, community engagement, technological advancements, and social impact, readers gain insights into the uniqueness of FedoraCoin within the cryptocurrency landscape.

1. Socially-Focused Mission: One of the key unique aspects of FedoraCoin is its socially-focused mission. This section delves into FedoraCoin's vision to leverage cryptocurrency for social good. It explores initiatives such as charitable donations, community-driven projects, and philanthropic endeavors supported by FedoraCoin. It highlights how FedoraCoin's community actively engages in social causes, creating a unique sense of purpose and impact.

2. Tipping Culture and Microtransactions: FedoraCoin popularized the concept of tipping within the cryptocurrency community. This section examines how FedoraCoin facilitated a culture of microtransactions, enabling users to tip and reward content creators, service providers, and community members. It explores the impact of tipping on community engagement, content monetization, and fostering a supportive ecosystem.

3. Community Governance and Decision-Making: FedoraCoin distinguishes itself through its community-driven governance model. This section discusses how the FedoraCoin community actively participates in decision-making processes, including project development, feature

enhancements, and strategic planning. It explores the decentralized nature of governance within FedoraCoin and the mechanisms employed to ensure transparency and inclusivity.

4. Innovative Applications and Partnerships: FedoraCoin stands out through its innovative applications and partnerships. This section showcases unique use cases and real-world applications of FedoraCoin beyond traditional transactions. It examines partnerships with businesses, platforms, and organizations that integrate FedoraCoin into their systems, creating new opportunities for adoption and utility.

5. Technical Advancements and Features: FedoraCoin introduces technical advancements and features that differentiate it from other cryptocurrencies. This section explores the technical aspects of FedoraCoin's blockchain, including its consensus algorithm, transaction speed, scalability, and privacy features. It discusses how these technical advancements enhance FedoraCoin's usability and address specific use case requirements.

6. Active and Engaged Community: The FedoraCoin community plays a vital role in its uniqueness. This section delves into the passionate and engaged community surrounding FedoraCoin, discussing the active involvement of community members in promoting, supporting, and expanding the ecosystem. It examines community-driven initiatives, educational resources, and events that foster collaboration and growth.

7. Social Media Integration and Awareness: FedoraCoin distinguishes itself through its integration with social media platforms. This section explores how FedoraCoin leverages social media channels to raise

awareness, engage with the community, and promote adoption. It discusses strategies employed to leverage the power of social media for the growth and visibility of FedoraCoin.

Conclusion: FedoraCoin possesses unique aspects that differentiate it from other cryptocurrencies. Through its socially-focused mission, tipping culture, community governance, innovative applications, technical advancements, engaged community, and social media integration, FedoraCoin creates a distinct identity within the cryptocurrency landscape. By understanding these unique aspects, readers gain insights into FedoraCoin's strengths, potential for impact, and its ability to carve out a niche within the broader crypto ecosystem.

Summary of key findings and insights

Introduction: Throughout this comprehensive exploration of various cryptocurrencies, including TrumpCoin, Pepecash, Coinye, 42 Coin, and FedoraCoin, we have delved into their backgrounds, technical features, market performance, and unique aspects. In this final subtopic, we summarize the key findings and insights gathered from each chapter, providing readers with a comprehensive overview of the cryptocurrency landscape and its evolving nature.

1. Understanding the Historical Significance: By examining the history of cryptocurrencies, we gain a deeper understanding of their origins, development, and the challenges they have faced. The historical context provides valuable insights into the evolution of the cryptocurrency market and the factors that have shaped its trajectory.

2. Importance of Technical Features: The technical features of cryptocurrencies, such as the underlying blockchain technology, consensus algorithms, security measures, and scalability, play a crucial role in their functionality, adoption, and long-term sustainability. Understanding these technical aspects is essential for evaluating the potential of a cryptocurrency and its suitability for various use cases.

3. Market Performance and Volatility: Analyzing the market performance of cryptocurrencies allows us to assess their growth, adoption, and investor sentiment. We have observed the significant price fluctuations, volatility, and market cycles that cryptocurrencies experience, highlighting the speculative nature of the market and the influence of external factors.

4. Unique Aspects and Use Cases: Each cryptocurrency examined in this book has its own unique aspects and use cases that set it apart from others. Whether it's the social focus of FedoraCoin, the integration with the crypto art community in Pepecash, or the community-driven governance model of Coinye, these unique features contribute to the overall ecosystem and attract different types of users and investors.

5. Community Engagement and Collaboration: The active engagement of communities surrounding cryptocurrencies is vital for their growth, development, and adoption. The power of a supportive and passionate community can drive innovation, foster partnerships, and promote widespread awareness and acceptance of a cryptocurrency.

6. Legal and Regulatory Challenges: Cryptocurrencies have faced various legal and regulatory challenges, including issues related to compliance, security, fraud, and government scrutiny. Understanding these challenges and the approaches taken by different cryptocurrencies to navigate the regulatory landscape is essential for assessing their long-term viability.

7. Impact on Financial Systems and Society: Cryptocurrencies have the potential to disrupt traditional financial systems, empower individuals, promote financial inclusion, and enable innovative applications. They also raise questions about privacy, security, and the future of money. Exploring the impact of cryptocurrencies on financial systems and society helps us grasp their transformative potential.

Conclusion: In conclusion, our exploration of various cryptocurrencies has provided valuable insights into their backgrounds, technical features, market performance, and unique aspects. We have witnessed the dynamic nature of the cryptocurrency market, characterized by innovation, volatility, and regulatory challenges. Key findings include the importance of understanding historical context, evaluating technical features, assessing market performance, recognizing unique aspects, engaging communities, navigating legal challenges, and envisioning the impact on financial systems and society.

As the cryptocurrency landscape continues to evolve, it is crucial to stay informed, adapt to changes, and critically evaluate the opportunities and risks associated with these digital assets. By embracing a multidimensional understanding of cryptocurrencies, we can navigate this rapidly changing landscape and contribute to the ongoing evolution of the decentralized economy.

Implications and future directions for cryptocurrencies

Introduction: Throughout this comprehensive exploration of various cryptocurrencies, we have delved into their backgrounds, technical features, market performance, and unique aspects. In this final subtopic, we examine the implications of cryptocurrencies and discuss potential future directions for this rapidly evolving field. By considering the broader implications and envisioning the possibilities, we can gain insights into the transformative potential of cryptocurrencies and their impact on various sectors.

1. Financial and Economic Implications: Cryptocurrencies have the potential to disrupt traditional financial systems and reshape economic landscapes. They offer increased financial inclusivity, lower transaction costs, and the ability to bypass intermediaries. However, they also present challenges such as regulatory concerns, market volatility, and the need for scalability. Understanding the financial and economic implications of cryptocurrencies is crucial for individuals, businesses, and governments to navigate this new financial paradigm.

2. Decentralization and Trust: One of the fundamental principles of cryptocurrencies is decentralization, which aims to eliminate the need for centralized intermediaries and foster trust among participants. By utilizing blockchain technology and consensus mechanisms, cryptocurrencies enable peer-to-peer transactions and verifiable trust without relying on traditional institutions. The implications of decentralization and trust extend beyond finance and can potentially revolutionize various industries, including supply chain management, voting systems, and intellectual property.

3. Privacy and Security: Cryptocurrencies introduce new dimensions of privacy and security. While transactions are pseudonymous and recorded on a public ledger, the underlying technology provides cryptographic security. However, privacy concerns arise as transactions can be traced, and the balance between privacy and transparency becomes a topic of debate. Exploring the implications of privacy and security in cryptocurrencies is essential to address potential vulnerabilities and develop robust solutions.

4. Regulatory and Legal Landscape: The regulatory and legal landscape surrounding cryptocurrencies is still evolving. Governments and regulatory bodies worldwide are grappling with how to regulate and provide oversight while fostering innovation. Striking the right balance is crucial to ensure consumer protection, prevent illicit activities, and promote market stability. Analyzing the implications of regulation and potential legal frameworks is necessary to establish a conducive environment for cryptocurrencies to thrive.

5. Adoption and Mainstream Integration: Cryptocurrency adoption and mainstream integration are critical for their long-term success. The journey towards mass adoption involves overcoming barriers such as user experience, scalability, and education. Collaboration between industry players, governments, and educational institutions is necessary to facilitate the integration of cryptocurrencies into existing financial systems and promote widespread awareness and understanding.

6. Technological Advancements: The development of cryptocurrencies is intrinsically tied to technological advancements. Improvements in blockchain technology,

consensus algorithms, scalability solutions, and interoperability protocols have the potential to address existing limitations and unlock new possibilities. Exploring future technological advancements and their implications for cryptocurrencies is crucial for envisioning the next generation of decentralized systems.

7. Social and Environmental Impact: Cryptocurrencies have the potential to empower individuals and communities, particularly those underserved by traditional financial systems. They can facilitate cross-border remittances, promote financial inclusion, and enable access to financial services for the unbanked. Additionally, the environmental impact of cryptocurrencies, particularly those based on energy-intensive consensus mechanisms, raises concerns. Evaluating the social and environmental impact of cryptocurrencies is essential to ensure a sustainable and equitable future.

Conclusion: In conclusion, cryptocurrencies present significant implications and hold the potential for transformative change across various domains. Understanding the financial, economic, technological, regulatory, and social implications is crucial for navigating the complex landscape of cryptocurrencies. Looking ahead, the future of cryptocurrencies depends on addressing challenges, fostering innovation, enhancing user experience, promoting regulatory clarity, and building trust. By considering the implications and envisioning future directions, we can actively shape the trajectory of cryptocurrencies and harness their transformative power for the benefit of individuals, businesses, and society as a whole.

Final thoughts and recommendations

Introduction: As we conclude this comprehensive exploration of cryptocurrencies, it is important to reflect on the key findings and insights we have gained throughout our journey. In this final subtopic, we provide our final thoughts and offer recommendations for individuals, businesses, and policymakers as they navigate the evolving world of cryptocurrencies. By considering the opportunities and challenges, we can provide guidance on how to leverage the potential of cryptocurrencies while mitigating risks.

1. Embrace the Potential of Cryptocurrencies: Cryptocurrencies have emerged as a disruptive force with the potential to transform various sectors. Embracing their potential involves recognizing the benefits they offer, such as financial inclusivity, lower transaction costs, and increased efficiency. By understanding the unique features and capabilities of cryptocurrencies, individuals and businesses can explore innovative use cases and harness their transformative power.

2. Educate Yourself and Promote Awareness: Cryptocurrencies operate on complex technologies and principles. It is crucial for individuals to educate themselves about the fundamentals of cryptocurrencies, blockchain technology, and the risks involved. Additionally, promoting awareness and providing accessible educational resources can help dispel misconceptions and foster a better understanding of cryptocurrencies among the general public.

3. Exercise Caution and Due Diligence: While cryptocurrencies present significant opportunities, they also come with risks. It is important for individuals and businesses to exercise caution and conduct thorough due diligence before engaging in cryptocurrency-related

activities. This includes researching projects, understanding the associated risks, and adopting best practices for securing digital assets, such as using hardware wallets and implementing strong security measures.

4. Diversify Investment Portfolios: Cryptocurrencies are highly volatile assets, and their market performance can be unpredictable. To mitigate risk, individuals and investors should consider diversifying their investment portfolios by including a mix of traditional assets and cryptocurrencies. Diversification can help balance risk and potentially maximize returns over the long term.

5. Foster Collaboration and Partnerships: The potential of cryptocurrencies can be further realized through collaboration and partnerships. Businesses and organizations across industries can explore opportunities to integrate cryptocurrencies into their existing systems, collaborate on blockchain projects, and leverage the benefits of decentralized networks. By fostering collaboration, we can unlock innovative solutions and drive widespread adoption.

6. Advocate for Clear Regulatory Frameworks: The regulatory landscape surrounding cryptocurrencies is still evolving. Policymakers should work towards establishing clear and balanced regulatory frameworks that protect consumers, foster innovation, and promote market stability. Collaborative efforts between governments, industry participants, and regulatory bodies are essential to develop coherent and globally coordinated regulatory approaches.

7. Support Research and Development: Cryptocurrencies are continuously evolving, and ongoing research and development are vital to drive innovation and address existing challenges. Governments, academic institutions, and industry players should support research

initiatives that focus on enhancing blockchain technology, scalability solutions, privacy features, and security measures. This will contribute to the overall growth and maturation of the cryptocurrency ecosystem.

Conclusion: In conclusion, the world of cryptocurrencies is dynamic and full of opportunities, but it also presents challenges that require careful navigation. By embracing the potential of cryptocurrencies, educating oneself and promoting awareness, exercising caution, diversifying investment portfolios, fostering collaboration, advocating for clear regulatory frameworks, and supporting research and development, we can lay the foundation for a thriving and sustainable cryptocurrency ecosystem.

Cryptocurrencies have the potential to reshape financial systems, empower individuals, drive innovation, and foster economic growth. However, their successful integration into mainstream society requires collective effort, responsible actions, and ongoing dialogue between stakeholders. By adopting a balanced and informed approach, we can navigate the complexities of cryptocurrencies and unlock their transformative power for the benefit of individuals, businesses, and society as a whole.

THE END

<h1 style="text-align:center">Key Terms and Definitions</h1>

To help you better understand the language and concepts related to aging and older adults, below you will find a list of key terms and their definitions.

1. Cryptocurrency: A digital or virtual form of currency that uses cryptography for secure financial transactions, control the creation of additional units, and verify the transfer of assets. Cryptocurrencies operate on decentralized networks called blockchains.

2. SHA-256: Secure Hash Algorithm 256-bit is a cryptographic hash function used by Bitcoin and many other cryptocurrencies. It converts data into a fixed-size string of characters, providing data integrity and security.

3. ATH: ATH stands for "All-Time High" and refers to the highest price or value that a cryptocurrency has ever reached in its history.

4. TrumpCoin: TrumpCoin is a cryptocurrency that was launched in 2016 with the aim of supporting the political agenda of Donald Trump, the former President of the United States.

5. Counterparty: Counterparty is a platform built on top of the Bitcoin blockchain that enables the creation and management of digital assets, smart contracts, and decentralized applications (DApps).

6. Pepecash: Pepecash is a cryptocurrency that originated from the Pepe the Frog internet meme. It was launched on the Counterparty platform and gained popularity within the crypto art community.

7. Coinye: Coinye, also known as Coinye West, was a short-lived cryptocurrency launched in 2014, inspired by the rapper Kanye West. It aimed to create a more approachable and mainstream-friendly cryptocurrency.

8. Scrypt: Scrypt is a cryptographic algorithm used in many cryptocurrencies, including Litecoin. It is designed to be memory-intensive and requires a large amount of memory to perform mining operations.

9. 42 Coin: 42 Coin is a cryptocurrency that was launched in 2014 with the goal of being the most valuable and rarest cryptocurrency in the world. It is known for its limited supply of only 42 coins.

10. FedoraCoin: FedoraCoin, also known as Tips, is a cryptocurrency that was launched in 2014. It aims to promote community-driven tipping and microtransactions on social media platforms.

11. USD: USD refers to the United States Dollar, which is the fiat currency of the United States and is widely used as a benchmark for measuring the value of cryptocurrencies.

12. ATH: ATH stands for "All-Time High" and refers to the highest price or value that a cryptocurrency has ever reached in its history.

13. Market Performance: Market performance refers to the overall performance of a cryptocurrency in terms of price movements, trading volume, market capitalization, and its position in the cryptocurrency market.

14. Legal Issues and Controversies: Legal issues and controversies pertain to the legal challenges, regulatory concerns, and controversies surrounding a particular cryptocurrency. This includes issues related to compliance, security, fraud, and the regulatory environment.

15. Community and Use Cases: Community and use cases refer to the user community built around a cryptocurrency and the various applications and real-world use cases for which the cryptocurrency is being utilized. This

includes areas such as payments, decentralized applications, and specific industries where the cryptocurrency finds utility.

16. Implications: Implications refer to the potential consequences or impacts that arise from the adoption and integration of cryptocurrencies into existing financial systems and societal structures. These implications can be economic, social, technological, or regulatory in nature.

17. Future Directions: Future directions pertain to the potential paths and developments that cryptocurrencies may take in the future. This includes advancements in technology, regulatory changes, market trends, and the evolution of use cases and applications.

18. Recommendations: Recommendations are suggested actions or strategies that individuals, businesses, and policymakers can follow to navigate the cryptocurrency landscape effectively. These recommendations aim to maximize opportunities while mitigating risks and promoting responsible adoption and usage of cryptocurrencies.

Supporting Materials

Introduction

Antonopoulos, A. M. (2014). Mastering Bitcoin: Unlocking Digital Cryptocurrencies. O'Reilly Media, Inc.

Chapter 1

TrumpCoin website. (n.d.). Retrieved from http://trumpcoin.com/

CoinMarketCap. (n.d.). TrumpCoin (TRUMP) price, charts, market cap, and other metrics. Retrieved from https://coinmarketcap.com/currencies/trumpcoin/

Chapter 2

Counterparty. (n.d.). Retrieved from https://counterparty.io/

CoinMarketCap. (n.d.). PepeCash (PEPECASH) price, charts, market cap, and other metrics. Retrieved from https://coinmarketcap.com/currencies/pepecash/

Chapter 3

Coinye West. (n.d.). Retrieved from https://en.bitcoin.it/wiki/Coinye_West

CoinMarketCap. (n.d.). Coinye (COYE) price, charts, market cap, and other metrics. Retrieved from https://coinmarketcap.com/currencies/coinye/

Chapter 4

42 Coin. (n.d.). Retrieved from https://42-coin.org/

CoinMarketCap. (n.d.). 42-coin (42) price, charts, market cap, and other metrics. Retrieved from https://coinmarketcap.com/currencies/42-coin/

Chapter 5

FedoraCoin. (n.d.). Retrieved from https://www.fedoracoin.top/

CoinMarketCap. (n.d.). FedoraCoin (TIPS) price, charts, market cap, and other metrics. Retrieved from https://coinmarketcap.com/currencies/fedoracoin/
Conclusion
Nakamoto, S. (2008). Bitcoin: A Peer-to-Peer Electronic Cash System. Retrieved from https://bitcoin.org/bitcoin.pdf
Popper, N. (2016). Digital Gold: Bitcoin and the Inside Story of the Misfits and Millionaires Trying to Reinvent Money. HarperCollins.